Fawzi kept the Makarov aimed at Katz's chest

"I feel as if we've hated each other for years," the terrorist colonel said. "Now we finally meet. Take out your gun slowly and drop it on the floor."

Katz reached for the holstered Eagle with his left hand. "This prosthetic arm is a bit clumsy," he said. "I'm not certain I can...."

"I'm getting impatient, cripple," Fawzi warned.

"Your threats don't worry me," Katz remarked, clamping the hook around the butt of the gun. "You make too many mistakes."

Suddenly Katz thrust his right arm forward, gripping the Eagle pistol. The curved steel "hand" pulled the trigger before the startled colonel could react, blasting a hole between Fawzi's eyes.

"That," Katz said, "was your last mistake."

Mack Bolan's
PHOENIX FORCE

Mack Bolan's
ABLE TEAM

PHOENIX FORCE
Return to Armageddon

Gar Wilson

A GOLD EAGLE BOOK FROM
WORLDWIDE

TORONTO · NEW YORK · LONDON · PARIS
AMSTERDAM · STOCKHOLM · HAMBURG
ATHENS · MILAN · TOKYO · SYDNEY

First edition May 1984

ISBN 0-373-61311-3

Special thanks and acknowledgment to
William Fieldhouse for his contributions to this work.

Copyright © 1984 by Worldwide Library.
Philippine copyright 1984. Australian copyright 1984.

All rights reserved. Except for use in any review, the
reproduction or utilization of this work in whole or in part
in any form by any electronic, mechanical or other means,
now known or hereafter invented, including xerography,
photocopying and recording, or in any information storage
or retrieval system, is forbidden without the permission
of the publisher, Worldwide Library, 225 Duncan Mill Road,
Don Mills, Ontario, Canada M3B 3K9.

All the characters in this book have no existence outside the
imagination of the author and have no relation whatsoever to
anyone bearing the same name or names. They are not even
distantly inspired by any individual known or unknown to the
author, and all the incidents are pure invention.

The Worldwide Library trademark consisting of the words
GOLD EAGLE is registered in the United States Patent
Office and in the Canada Trade Marks Office. The Gold Eagle
design trademark, the Executioner series design trademark,
the Phoenix Force design trademark, the globe design
trademark, and the Worldwide design trademark consisting
of the word WORLDWIDE in which the letter "O" is
represented by a depiction of a globe, are trademarks
of Worldwide Library.

Printed in Canada

1

The congregation of fanatics stood in the assembly hall, silently waiting for the old man. The scent of jasmine incense filled the hall, all but concealing the pungent odor of hashish. Symbols were engraved on the walls. To those not initiated to the Order, these emblems were rather crude stars and interlocked circles, yet the symbols had great meaning to the initiated.

The followers of the Order stood rigidly, like soldiers about to be reviewed by an inspector general. Indeed, they were soldiers—totally dedicated to their cult and its messiah.

The old man, the messiah, emerged from behind a beaded curtain. Dressed in a white djellaba—robe—with a matching *keffiyeh*—Arab headdress—and a red sash around his waist, Hassan the Sheik of the Holy Order majestically walked across a raised platform to a throne. He sat in the royal chair, thoughtfully stroked his flowing white beard and gazed at his followers through coal-black eyes.

Hassan was pleased with his disciples. They were the elite of the order, the true devotees. They were, according to the prophet Hassan, the hands of Allah, chosen to carry out the will of God on earth.

Every member of the congregation wore a white *brussa*—shirt—and trousers with a red sash and boots. A crest was sewn into the breast of each *brussa*—a heart-shaped symbol with two vees breaking the top and bottom of the emblem.

"My children," Hassan began, "the infidels continue to increase in number. They surround us and threaten to contaminate our pure belief with their poisonous sin. We are surrounded by the Jews and Christians and those who call themselves Islams and claim to follow the will of Allah."

"Hassan and Allah are one," the followers chanted. "His voice is the only true word of Allah."

The old man held up a hand for silence. The command was instantly obeyed.

"As you know," he continued, "the prime minister of Israel has again been stricken by a heart illness. Allah punishes this fiend who must die many times to compensate for his wrongs."

"Death to all infidels," the crowd called out in unison.

"And it shall be death," Hassan said. "The destruction of the heretics is at hand. The Israeli prime minister has been rendered helpless and placed in a vulnerable position for a reason. It is part of Allah's plan to annihilate those who worship false religions. Only we who know the Truth will remain to be rewarded for our devotion."

The congregation was unable to bottle its emotion. An excited murmur filled the hall. The prophet had promised that the great day would arrive in their lifetime and now it was upon them. The hands of Allah did not doubt their master's word. They had been to paradise. They had actually seen the green valley and drank from the rivers of wine. None of them feared death and none questioned the word of Hassan.

"I will allow Basi Majid to explain the rest," Hassan announced as he clapped his hands.

Jemal, Hassan's personal manservant and bodyguard, appeared. Jemal, a large black man, was a eunuch slave. As an infant, he was castrated so that he could not be led astray by women; his tongue was cut out so he could not utter blasphemy or lies; and he was illiterate, unable to read or write untruth.

Jemal was considered "pure" in his ignorance. Hassan had molded him since childhood, personally supervising the boy's religious education and vigorous physical training program. The success of the latter was obvious. Jemal's body bulged with heavily developed muscles.

The eunuch wore white silk breeches, red slippers and a scimitar thrust in a scarlet sash. He carried a large silver tray with a dome lid and marched to a small table covered by a crimson cloth. Hassan nodded at his servant. Jemal carefully placed the platter on the table.

"You all know that Basi Majid is one of my most trusted subchiefs," Hassan said. "He is a true believer who has been part of the Most Holy Order for many years. Today he achieved the ultimate glory. Allah told me it was time for Basi to join Him in paradise. So I ordered Jemal to dispatch Basi to the next world."

Hassan gestured with his hand and Jemal promptly grabbed the lid and removed it from the tray. The congregation stared silently at the face of Basi Majid. The man's head was in the center of the platter, surrounded by blood. His eyes gazed at the ceiling without blinking. His open mouth was stained with scarlet.

"Basi was chosen to join Allah," Hassan explained, "and to deliver a message from our Lord in paradise."

The congregation continued to stare at the man's head on the tray. Then a gasp erupted from the onlookers as they saw Basi's eyelids flutter. Slowly, the head's lips moved.

"Brothers," a voice from Basi's head called out hoarsely. "Allah has granted me salvation for loyal service to the great prophet Hassan. Follow his word, for it is the only path to paradise."

"Lord Hassan is Allah's only true prophet," the congregation cried. "We shall obey the Law. We shall obey the word of Lord Hassan."

"There is more, brothers," Basi declared. "The great war of the infidels is about to happen. We, the true believers, are to be the catalyst for this conflict. The Israeli leader's death will be the beginning of the last holy war. The great

Lord Hassan will tell you how this shall come to pass. Follow his word and victory shall be ours. It is the will of Allah.''

LATER THAT EVENING Hassan relaxed on a comfortable sofa with his bare feet propped on some pillows. Nasser Fawzi sat across from the old man. Jemal poured jasmine tea for the pair.

"*Alf Shukreh,* Jemal," Hassan told his servant. "Now fetch the dates and yogurt."

Jemal nodded and turned to carry out the command. Hassan saluted Fawzi with his teacup.

"To success, my friend," he said. "Or should I call you comrade, Colonel?"

"Just colonel," Fawzi replied dryly. "You are not a member of the United Arab Front, so there is no reason for you to address me as comrade."

"Very well, Colonel," Hassan said, shrugging.

Fawzi wore a khaki uniform and web belt with a Makarov 9mm pistol on his hip, but he was not a soldier in a regular army. The tall Syrian had appointed himself colonel when he formed the United Arab Front, a small organization that consisted of some of the worst fanatical terrorists in the Middle East. They were renegades with a reputation for being mad dogs, and they were so radical even Arafat and Khaddafi did not want to be associated with them. However, Fawzi had found an ally in Hassan and his Holy Order. And, he had found that the old man's followers were even more fanatical than the UAF.

Hassan was not as old as he appeared to be. He had dyed his hair white to suit his image as the Lord of the Holy Order. Forty-five years old and reasonably fit, Hassan purposely tried to look at least twenty years older then he was. He was a showman and knew how to make an impression on his men.

"You put on quite a performance today, Essiyid Hassan," Fawzi remarked as he fished a pack of cigarettes from his pocket.

"I know my children," Hassan replied, opening a small teak box. "I know their superstitions and the legends that comprise their religion. I've got some Turkish cigarettes here, Colonel. Would you care for one? They're made of the finest tobacco in the world."

"*Just* tobacco?" Fawzi asked suspiciously.

"I'd have no reason to drug you, Colonel," Hassan assured him.

"I'll smoke my own," Fawzi told him, shaking a cigarette from its pack.

"You must learn to trust me, Colonel. After all, I trust you to pay me in full—although I've received only a fourth of my fee thus far."

"You'll get the rest," Fawzi said. "And you agreed to the partial payment until the completion of your mission."

"I'm not complaining, Colonel," Hassan told him. "But make certain the rest of the payment is in diamonds. Small stones. Uncut if possible."

"I understand. Diamonds are an international

form of currency. You may decide to leave the Middle East abruptly.''

"That may be a wise choice of action," Hassan confessed. "Considering what will probably happen in the very near future.''

"Probably?" Fawzi frowned. "You guaranteed success of your assignment.''

"My assignment will be successful, Colonel," Hassan promised. "But no one can predict how the Israelis will react.''

"The Jews will react exactly the way we want them to," the colonel said. "When they do, it will enhance your image as a prophet because the holy war you spoke of will then begin.''

"The will of Allah," Hassan joked as he plucked a cigarette from the box.

"Doesn't it bother you to constantly play the role of a holy man?" Fawzi asked, unable to conceal his contempt.

"The worse part is having to appear to be divine in the presence of my followers," Hassan explained, lighting his cigarette. "I cannot smoke, drink, eat or even spit when they can see me. God sustains me in all things.''

"But you manipulate these men," Fawzi said. "You use them to achieve your own selfish, greedy goals.''

"Really, Colonel," Hassan laughed. "You've hired me to do a job and now you question my ethics? That is quite amusing since your organization is nothing more than a gang of murderers. . . .''

"We're fighting to liberate our people from oppression," Fawzi insisted.

"Save your Marxist rhetoric for your comrades, Colonel," Hassan replied. "We both know that *you* manipulate and use your men just as I do."

"I do not claim to be speaking for God."

Hassan merely laughed.

Fawzi realized his criticism of Hassan was absurd. He was a Communist, an atheist. And Fawzi hated men like Hassan, men who preached from the Koran and the Bible. Religion had kept the Arabic nations from endorsing communism. Until they all united under the red banner, the Arab world could never hope to destroy the Jews or drive out the imperialistic Westerners from the Middle East.

But Fawzi believed the end justifies the means, so he had no qualms about Hassan's role in the mission. He decided to change the subject.

"That talking head trick was very effective. How did you do it?"

"Why don't you ask Basi?" Hassan suggested.

Five minutes later, Jemal escorted Basi Majid into the room. The bearded head was mounted on a stocky body, remarkably recovered from his decapitation. Basi grinned at Hassan and Fawzi.

"Colonel Fawzi is curious about today's performance, Basi. Explain it to him."

"Simple enough," Basi told the UAF commander. "I was hidden under the table, concealed by the tablecloth. Jemal carried in the tray that was covered by the lid, so no one knew it was really empty.''

"Actually it did contain some goat's blood,'' Hassan interrupted. "The tray is hoop shaped with a hollow center.''

"So Jemal put the platter on the table and Basi simply poked his head up through a hole in the table top,'' Fawzi said, guessing the rest. "Very clever.''

"A variation of an old trick.'' Hassan shrugged. "My namesake, the original Hassan who founded the order centuries ago, used a similar technique to convince his followers that he could control life and death.''

"An effective illusion,'' Fawzi stated. "But how will you explain Basi's resurrection to the others?''

"That won't be necessary,'' Hassan replied.

"I'll have to remain in hiding here in the secret chambers,'' Basi told Fawzi. "Then, when the time is right, I'll be smuggled out of the country.''

"That plan is too risky, Basi,'' Hassan sighed. "Another choice of action must be taken. Jemal, see to Basi's departure.''

The startled Basi's eyes expanded with fear. "What do you...?''

Jemal seized the man from behind. His left hand clawed into Basi's bearded chin, pressing his jaw shut, while the slave's other fist crashed into Basi's right temple. Basi Majid's senseless body slumped limply into Jemal's arms.

"What will happen to him?" Fawzi asked as he watched Jemal drag his unconscious victim from the room.

"Basi has outlived his usefulness," Hassan replied.

"Basi was one of your most trusted men," Fawzi remarked. "You knew him for years, yet you don't hesitate to kill him just to ensure his silence?"

"A dead man tells no secrets, Colonel," Hassan answered. "And Basi can now serve one last function. His decapitated head will be displayed to my followers once more. This time they'll be able to examine it in detail. Of course, it will no longer speak since the holy message Allah placed in Basi's mouth has already been delivered. Seeing that the head of Basi Majid has indeed been separated from his body will further convince my children that they did indeed witness a miracle this day."

"I wonder," the colonel began, "is it wise for me to trust a man who can kill a friend so casually?"

"Friendship is a commodity to be used and discarded when it is no longer needed. I am interested in two things—profit and power. If you continue to be useful to me in my quest for these goals, then you have no reason to fear me, Colonel."

"I think we understand each other," Fawzi told him, saluting Hassan with his teacup. "Success at any price."

"A fine motto," Hassan said. "Words to live by...."

The sound of Jemal's scimitar carried into the parlor. The two men heard the blade violently slash through air before it chopped into flesh. Hassan frowned when he heard Basi Majid's head strike the floor.

"Or die by," he added philosophically.

2

First Lieutenant Arthur Goldblum was grateful for the air conditioner. He had been an Israeli citizen for almost ten years, yet he had never adjusted to the heat.

Goldblum, a Jew, had grown up in the Bronx. His father had owned a small grocery store in a lower-middle-class neighborhood.

Goldblum had been an Airborne Ranger in the United States Army in Nam. He saw plenty of action in history's dirtiest war. But most of the battles he was involved in never received much press coverage; their significance mattered only to the men who fought them.

Like thousands of other American servicemen, Arthur Goldblum had returned from Vietnam to discover hostile territory was not confined to the jungles of Southeast Asia. Americans did not welcome him home with parades and flowery speeches. Instead, they shunned him like a leper.

Opponents of the war hated him because he fought instead of fleeing to Canada. Supporters of the war regarded him as a wimp because his generation had failed to defeat a little fifth-rate

Communist country. Everyone seemed to regard him as either a war-loving psycho or a coward.

Arthur Goldblum decided to leave the United States and move to a new country—one in which he was automatically a citizen by birthright.

Israel is a country surrounded by hostile nations. It is, by necessity, a militaristic country. All eighteen-year-olds are required to spend three years in active military service, and they remain in the reserves until the age of fifty-five. Thus, Israel welcomed experienced warriors. Goldblum had found a new home.

He joined the elite Israeli Independent Paratrooper Detachment and rapidly rose through the ranks. He received a commission and became an officer. He also received a top-security clearance and served duty attached to the Sheruth Modiin, the Israeli Military Intelligence Department. Lieutenant Goldblum participated in several clandestine raids into Lebanon and Syria.

Lieutenant Goldblum had earned the trust and confidence of his superiors. He had been chosen by Lieutenant Colonel Zavarj to be a unit commander of a special security-guard force that was protecting the prime minister while he recovered from a heart attack at the Straus Health Centre in Tel Aviv.

The Sheruth Modiin had blocked off the entire sixteenth floor of the east wing and stationed soldiers at the elevator and stairs. No one was permitted to enter the area without a special identification badge complete with a photograph and a code number. All personnel who entered the wing had to pass a checkpoint.

The third checkpoint on the sixteenth floor was Goldblum's responsibility. He sat at a field desk by the elevators with a clipboard full of names and code numbers.

Two commandos stood guard in front of room number twenty-six. They were highly trained professional soldiers, well armed with Uzi machine pistols and side arms. Every man also carried a small two-way radio on his belt in case reinforcements were needed.

Like the other soldiers in the unit, Goldblum wore a practical green fatigue uniform with a red beret of the Israeli Paratroopers. He was the only officer on the sixteenth floor. Two silver bars were tacked to his beret, the insignia of a first lieutenant—identical to the insignia of a captain in the American Army.

Goldblum, eager to be off duty, glanced at his wristwatch. He would still be restricted to the hospital, of course—everyone was locked in the building until the prime minister was ready to leave. Still, Goldblum was bored behind the field desk.

The indicator light above the elevator switched on. Goldblum noticed the lift was rising from the tenth floor. Most of the personnel authorized to be in the restricted sixteenth-floor area came directly from the lobby, so the lieutenant was surprised when the elevator stopped at his station.

The doors opened with an electrical hum and two men dressed in hospital whites rolled a metal cart out of the elevator. Goldblum stared suspiciously at the sheet that covered an obscure shape on the top shelf of the cart.

"*Boker tov,* Lieutenant," one of the orderlies greeted.

"*Shalom,*" Goldblum replied without enthusiasm as he rose from his desk. "Are you both authorized in this area?"

"Yes we are, sir," the same orderly said. "Dr. Ravitch sent us to change the prime minister's bed sheets and the bedpan."

"I was not notified about this," Goldblum said, scanning over their ID badges.

Both orderlies were small, swarthy men with olive complexions. Probably Arabs, Goldblum thought.

The numerals on the badges matched the code numbers for two orderlies named Hunada and Khalil. The photos were smudged, but they seemed to resemble the pair. The lieutenant relaxed a bit and placed the clipboard on the desk beside his Uzi as he approached the pair.

"Will you remove the sheet, *buvaka sha?*" he asked, but his voice carried a tone of authority that made it clear he was not making a request.

"Of course, Lieutenant." The Arab pulled back the sheet.

Goldblum looked down at several bedpans, a stack of neatly folded towels and a Russian PPSH-41 submachine gun.

"Shit," Goldblum gasped as he made a desperate grab for the Eagle pistol in his shoulder holster.

He was not fast enough. One of the orderlies grabbed Goldblum's wrist, preventing him from drawing the gun. The Arab's other hand produced a dagger from under his white jacket. He punched the double-edged blade into Goldblum's solar plexus, driving the steel point up into his heart.

Sharp burning pain filled Lieutenant Goldblum's chest as he stared into the face of his murderer. The Arab's eyes twinkled and a smile of satisfaction burst across his dark features. Yet his pleasure was not sadistic as he whispered gently in Hebrew.

"The pain will be brief."

It was. Goldblum was dead before he slumped to the tile floor.

The two paratroopers stationed in front of room twenty-six immediately unslung their Uzi subguns. However, the other Arab had already gathered up the PPS and aimed it at the soldiers. The Soviet-made chatterbox sprayed 7.62mm slugs into the guards.

Bullets ripped through flesh and muscle, mashing vital organs. Blood soaked fatigue shirts as the Israeli commandos tumbled to the floor. Their lifeless bodies rolled across the corridor, propelled by more full-auto projectiles. The machine gunner continued to fire the PPS as he approached the slain Israelis.

The other Arab left his knife buried in Gold-blum's chest and took the dead lieutenant's Uzi from the field desk. His partner exhausted the ammunition from his PPS and reached under his jacket for a fresh magazine.

Neither man spoke, for they knew what to do next. The stench of cordite filled their nostrils, and strands of gray gun smoke drifted through the hallway. Their ears rang and their skulls throbbed painfully from the effects of gunfire within a confined area.

Their plan of action was simple and brutally direct.

They rushed to room twenty-six and kicked in the door. Inside, a lone figure lay in a bed surrounded by a transparent plastic veil.

"Allah akbar," they cried as they aimed their weapons at the figure.

Twin streams of full-auto missiles tore through the flimsy oxygen tent. Bullets struck the motionless figure on the bed, smashing into its torso and shattering its skull.

They were still firing at the helpless figure when a trio of Israeli Paratroopers burst into the corridor from the emergency stairwell.

The soldiers opened fire. Nine-millimeter lead hornets with copper jackets struck the Arab gunmen. The impact of the Uzi rounds sent one of the killers sprawling across the floor. His PPS flew from his grasp, his left arm dangled from a bullet-shredded shoulder.

The other Arab turned his gun on the paratroopers. He received several 9mm slugs in the chest before he could trigger the weapon. His body was hurtled backward. He crashed to the floor in a lifeless, bloodied heap.

"Hold your fire," Captain Rosen ordered as he advanced toward the wounded Arab.

The smoking muzzles of their submachine guns pointed at the injured man, the paratroopers cautiously approached. The Arab gazed up at them, his face splattered with blood as the severed brachial artery in his ravaged shoulder continued to pump out his life fluids. Incredibly, the man smiled at his captors.

"Asha-du Allah ilaha illa Allah," the Arab declared, drawing a dagger from his belt.

"Drop it," Rosen ordered.

The assassin ignored him and thrust the knife under his own chin. The point of the blade stabbed through the soft flesh under his jawbone. A hard shove sent it upward, penetrating the roof of his mouth, piercing the brain.

"God of our fathers," Captain Rosen whispered as he watched the Arab's body twitch in death.

"What did he say before he killed himself?" one of the commandos who did not understand Arabic inquired.

"An Islamic proverb," Rosen answered. " 'I witness that there is no God but Allah.' "

"Captain," a voice called from the stairs.

Rosen turned to see a tall figure approaching. Dressed in a bush shirt and khaki trousers, he wore no insignia of rank, but Rosen recognized him. The man had curly black hair, graying at the temples, and a vivid white scar on his left cheek.

"Major Eytan," Rosen greeted. "We almost had a prisoner, but he chose to take his own life."

"Not until he and his comrade managed to kill three of our people," Eytan said bitterly.

Eytan entered room number twenty-six and gazed down at the tattered remains of the oxygen tent and the bullet-shattered body in the bed. He shook his head grimly.

"They shouldn't have been able to get this far, Captain," he stated.

"We'll find out how they did it, Major," Rosen assured him.

"And find out who they were," Eytan snapped. "By God, whoever sent them will pay dearly for this."

He stepped forward and seized the oxygen tent, ripping it apart with an angry tug. Bits of flesh-colored plastic were scattered over the bed sheets. The figure's head lay beside its body. A glass eye bulged from its cracked socket, all that remained of the mannequin's features.

"The dummy was to serve as a decoy, Major," Captain Rosen remarked. "It succeeded to a degree."

"They shouldn't have gotten this far," Eytan repeated. "And the next time they'll make certain the real prime minister is the target."

"Maybe there won't be a next time," Rosen said.

"There will *always* be a next time, my young friend," Eytan said with a sigh.

3

Yakov Katzenelenbogen felt strangely uncomfortable as he entered the office. Perhaps he felt odd because he was wearing a uniform. It was the first time in five years he had donned his military garments, complete with campaign ribbons and medals won for valor. Pinned to his beret was the triple-fig-leaf emblem of a full colonel in the Israeli armed forces.

Perhaps he felt uneasy having been summoned into the office of the deputy director of the Central Institute for Intelligence and Special Missions—better known as Mossad.

But Katz was no stranger to the deputy director's office. The interior had changed over the years.

The face behind the desk was also different. Katz did not recognize the diminutive, dour, bald man who examined him. He glanced at the other two men who rose from their plastic scoop-backed chairs to face him.

"I've heard a good deal about you, Colonel Katzenelenbogen," the deputy director said. "It is a pleasure to meet you at last."

"Thank you, Director Geller," Katz replied,

although he realized the little man was being less than sincere.

Moshe Geller seemed disappointed when he saw Katz. Yakov could easily be mistaken for a college professor. He was in his mid-fifties, with iron-gray hair and a rather paunchy midsection. His face was dominated by gentle blue eyes that seemed to radiate patience and wisdom.

Only his right arm which had been amputated at the elbow, suggested he may have had any combat experience. Katz made no effort to conceal his handicap; in fact, he had emphasized it by folding up the empty sleeve and pinning it.

"I don't believe you've met these other gentlemen, Colonel," Geller said. "Lieutenant Colonel Ezra Zavarj of the Sheruth Modin and Major Uri Eytan from Mossad Special Missions Department."

Katz realized something important was happening. Clandestine organizations in every country seemed to form a rivalry with one another. That was true of the CIA and the FBI in the United States, the BND and the GFV in West Germany and even the Soviet KGB and the GRU. Israel was no exception. For military intelligence and Mossad to be working together, they had to be up against something big.

Yakov extended his left arm to shake hands with the two men. Zavarj was a wiry man with silver hair and a ready smile. Eytan was more somber. His eyes lingered on Katz's abbreviated right arm.

"I lost it in the Six Day War," Yakov told him. "I was lucky, many lost their lives." He did not mention that his son had been one of the casualties of that conflict.

"The Six Day War was a very long time ago, Colonel," Eytan mused.

"Major," Geller began sternly, "Colonel Katzenelenbogen has been actively involved in warfare, espionage and antiterrorism since he was a teenager. He was in Europe with the Resistance fighters against the Nazis. He served in the Haganah against the British when Israel was still fighting for independence and continued with Mossad afterward. Technically, he has retired from our organization, but he has stayed in contact with us over the years and we've exchanged information in the past. In fact, you've received a fair amount of classified intelligence from this office, haven't you, Colonel?"

"And what have you done with that information, Colonel?" Eytan asked suspiciously.

"I've used it wisely," Katz replied.

"Colonel Katzenelenbogen has a fine record," Geller assured the others.

"How is it that you happen to be in Israel at this time, Colonel?" Eytan asked bluntly.

"I'm here to do some research for a book," Katz answered. "I'm working on a volume about Middle Eastern archaeology. I have a degree in that science, and I've written a good deal about it in the magazine *Archaeological Quarterly*."

"Not a terribly patriotic reason to be in our country," the major remarked.

"I'm sure you'll be even less pleased to know I have a dual citizenship for Israel and France. And over the past few years I've spent more time in Europe and the United States than in the Middle East. As a matter of fact, I'm thinking of giving up my French citizenship and becoming a U.S. citizen. I've never been given the third degree in America like I'm getting from you people right now."

"Colonel," Geller began in an apologetic tone.

"Let me finish," Katz insisted. "When I do return to the Middle East, it has usually been in connection with various international import-export businesses. I serve as a go-between for many of them because I have many connections in the Middle East and I speak Hebrew, Arabic, French, Russian, German and English, which allows me to communicate with virtually everyone I'm apt to do business with short of Kurdish street merchants."

"You've done business with Arabs?" Kavarj asked.

"Saudis and Egyptians mostly," Katz replied. "What's wrong with that?"

"You don't think much of being Jewish, do you, Colonel?" the major spat, glaring at him.

"I am a Jew," Katz stated. "But that doesn't mean I have to limit my business associates and personal friendships only to fellow Jews. There are some Jews I don't much care for, Major. For example, I'm not very fond of you and your integrity quiz.''

"Colonel," Geller sighed. "No one questions your loyalty, but please spare us this charade. We're well aware that your business trips are a cover for other activities. You've hardly retired from the world of espionage. In fact, you've been doing quite a bit of work for the Americans. Some sort of special antiterrorist unit, I believe?''

"I'm not at liberty to discuss that in detail," Katz stated.

Yakov Katzenelenbogen was in fact the unit commander of Phoenix Force, the world's top team of antiterrorists.

Phoenix Force had been formed by the legendary crime fighter Mack Bolan, sometimes called The Executioner. After his one-man war against the Mafia, Bolan, working for the U.S. president under the name of Colonel John Phoenix, waged a war against terrorism. To help him in his battle against international barbarians, he had personally selected five men—the best antiterrorist experts the free world had to offer—to serve as a new American foreign legion, a dynamite team of terrorist beaters.

Phoenix Force had lived up to all expectations. The five-man army had succeeded in ten incredible missions against some of the most insidious terrorist organizations and conspiracies in the shadowy history of evil. However, the situation at Bolan's Stony Man operations had changed drastically.

A devastating series of events had turned Bolan into a fugitive, wanted by virtually every intelligence network and law-enforcement agency throughout the world. The Executioner was once again a renegade on the lam, pitted against impossible odds.

There had been some danger that Phoenix Force would be disbanded after Bolan fell out of favor with the president. However, Hal Brognola, the Fed who had acted as the go-between for the White House and Stony Man, was officially in charge of Phoenix Force operations, and he convinced all concerned that Phoenix must continue to fly. The plug could still be pulled if the president changed his mind—a fact that worried Katz and his four teammates.

"I won't ask you to give away any information about your less-public activities," Geller assured Katz. "It doesn't concern us at this time. The fact is, you are an Israeli and you happen to be in the country right now. We may well need your expertise."

"I'm listening."

"Early this morning," the deputy director said, "there was an attempt to assassinate the prime minister. Major Eytan was stationed at the hospital when it occurred."

"Two men entered the restricted area," the major explained. "They wore ID badges taken from a pair of orderlies who were later found dead in a dumpster, their throats cut."

"Any information about the assassins?" Katz asked.

"They were both Egyptians," Zavarj replied grimly.

"Egyptians?" Katz said, frowning. "Are you certain they weren't carrying forged identification?"

"We're sure," Eytan confirmed. "Their passports are genuine. We checked names, fingerprints and dental files. They were both members of the United Arab Republic's Ground Forces."

"You're not suggesting this was an act of war by Egypt against Israel?" Katz inquired.

"Those two killers were Egyptian soldiers, not PLO terrorists," Geller said. "Perhaps President Mubarak has been making some covert agreements with Arafat or Khaddafi."

"Khaddafi?" Yakov shook his head. "That's absurd. Egypt has no more love for that Libyan lunatic than we do. Mubarak has done nothing to deserve such accusations. Since he became president of Egypt after the assassination of Anwar Sadat, Mubarak has upheld the peace treaty with Israel."

"The Egyptians are Arabs," Eytan said. "Don't forget that."

"I seem to recall it was President Sadat who first had the courage to come to Israel and offer to make peace," Katz snapped.

"I'm surprised you trust the Egyptians," Zavarj mused. "I wouldn't think you'd forget the Six Day War."

"I haven't," Katz assured him. "I haven't forgotten the Nazis, either, but I don't condemn West Germany for what Hitler did. Bitterness and hatred has been the scourge of the Middle East. All too often, Jews have been as guilty of this as the Arabs.''

''Yesterday's enemies can become today's friends,'' Geller remarked. ''But we know that everyone who claims friendship does not always speak the truth. We have to be certain whether the two Egyptian killers were just fanatics or if they were sent by their government.''

He turned to Katz. ''You have more experience in dealing with terrorism than anyone in this room. For this reason, Mossad wants to put you in charge of a committee of advisers to investigate this incident.''

''Committee of advisers?'' Katz said, laughing. ''That's nonsense. I've never been a paper pusher and I'm too old to start. Why don't you allow me to handle this in the manner I am accustomed to?''

''What do you have in mind, Colonel?''

''First of all,'' Katz began, ''the assassination attempt was done by terrorists.''

''How can you be sure?'' Zavarj demanded.

''Because I know how the bastards operate,'' Katz insisted. ''The Egyptians aren't stupid. They wouldn't have sent someone we could check so easily and trace the assassination to them if they were responsible. Someone is trying to set Israel and Egypt at each other's throats.''

''Can you prove this?'' Geller asked.

"If I have the right men to help me."

"All right," Geller decided, after some thought. "We'll let you try it your way. Major Eytan will help you select the men you'll need."

"I already know who I want to work with," Katz informed him. "I'll contact them as quickly as possible and have them fly to Israel immediately."

"You're getting foreigners instead of using Israeli commandos?" Eytan asked with surprise.

"But we've got the best antiterrorist section in the world," Zavarj insisted.

"They're very good," Yakov agreed. "But I want the very best. The four men I'm going to send for are exactly that. I stake my life on their ability."

"More than your life is at stake, Colonel," Geller told him. "The State of Israel may be in jeopardy."

"The state of the world..." Katz added grimly.

4

"I hate mucking about without knowing what the hell I'm doing," David McCarter muttered as he sullenly stared out the window of the Boeing 747.

"You've been doing it all your life," Rafael Encizo replied with a wry grin.

Encizo was disappointed when McCarter failed to counter the remark. The Englishman seldom missed an opportunity to exercise his caustic wit. McCarter was known for his sense of humor and the sharp tongue that accompanied it, yet he had been strangely quiet since boarding the plane at Montreal.

McCarter, Encizo and Keio Ohara had been at Gary Manning's home in Montreal. The Phoenix Force members had planned to journey north of the city to conduct a field exercise in wilderness survival.

But Manning had received a telephone call. The Canadian was surprised to hear Colonel Katzenelenbogen's voice.

"Get to Israel immediately," Katz said. "We can get everything we'll need at this end. I'll meet you and the others at the Ben Gurion International Airport."

"We'll be there," Manning answered, aware that Katz would not answer any questions on a telephone.

The four men had made reservations on the first available flight to Israel. Phoenix Force seldom used commercial airlines, yet under the circumstances it had been the fastest possible route. They sat together in the business class section, quietly discussing the situation.

All four men were very different from each other in appearance. McCarter stood six feet tall with a leanly muscled physique and a handsome face. A bundle of nervous energy, the SAS-trained Englishman thrived on adventure. In combat he was a fearless dynamo, totally committed to the success of the mission.

Encizo was shorter and stockier than McCarter. His good looks and ready smile covered a hard-nosed professional who had endured considerable misery and torment at the hands of Castro's regime. He was a cunning, often ruthless warrior who never backed down regardless of the odds.

Manning was a strong man. The Canadian workaholic committed himself to every task with bulldog determination and limitless endurance. An expert in demolitions and explosives, he had the cool head needed for such work and the courage to charge into battle and get the job done.

Ohara possessed the same qualities of bravery and devotion inherent in his samurai ancestors. More than six feet tall, the Japanese member of

Phoenix Force was a highly disciplined fighting machine, skilled in karate, judo and kendo sword fighting. An electronics genius and the youngest man on the team, he had proven to be one hundred percent reliable in combat.

"Katz had better have a bloody good excuse for this," McCarter stated as he gulped down his Coca-Cola.

"I don't like this either," Gary Manning said as he leafed through a Hebrew phrase book. "This mission hasn't been planned out."

"And Katz of all people was the one who called us," McCarter added. "Have you ever known him to use a bloody telephone to contact us about a mission?"

"I don't like going to an assignment with a minimum of personal equipment," Encizo stated. "The stuff we managed to smuggle on board won't do us a hell of a lot of good in a major firefight."

"We didn't even receive a briefing from Brognola," Manning said.

"Perhaps Brognola is not aware of this mission," Ohara remarked.

"Not aware of it?" Manning said, frowning. "But we're part of Stony Man. Our orders come from Brognola."

"Are you sure of that, Gary?" Encizo asked. "After what's happened, can we really be sure Stony Man is still in operation?"

"You're referring to what happened to Colonel Phoenix?" Ohara commented.

"Colonel Phoenix?" McCarter snorted. "Keio, we've always known who 'Colonel Phoenix' really was. Why play that game any longer?"

"The Executioner is a fugitive," Encizo added. "The whole goddamn world is after his head now."

"I see your point," Manning said. "Brognola and Mack Bolan go back quite a ways. The Fed was Bolan's secret ally when The Executioner was still fighting the Mafia. Since Bolan turned renegade, the White House might very well have decided to cut Brognola from the program as well."

"Or scrapped Stony Man all together," McCarter added. "One thing is certain; we're all walking on thin ice. The president is bound to be suspicious of the lot of us now. After all, Bolan chose us."

"Well, let's worry about all this crap later," Manning said. "Right now, I'm more interested in why the hell Katz wants us in Israel."

"Whatever it is," McCarter began, "the situation must be critical for Katz to violate security procedures in order to contact us directly."

"Maybe he's going to tell us we've been canned," Encizo joked.

Nobody laughed.

THE BOEING 747 TOUCHED DOWN at the Ben Gurion International Airport at 1120, Tel Aviv time. The four Phoenix Force warriors deplaned at gate thirteen. Katz was waiting to greet them.

The Israeli wore a white linen suit and a pair of pearl-gray gloves. The suit jacket concealed a compact .380-caliber Beretta automatic in a shoulder-holster rig, and the long sleeves and gloves covered the mechanical limb attached to the stump of Katz's right arm.

"I thought we were in Israel not on 'Fantasy Island,' " McCarter quipped when he saw Katz's white suit.

"I see you haven't changed," Yakov said, unable to resist a smile. "But I'm afraid instead of a fantasy, we might well have a nightmare on our hands. I'll explain later."

"Yeah," Manning stated. "And we've got some other questions for you, Yakov."

"I'm sure you do," the Israeli said.

He glanced at the carryon luggage the men had brought from the plane. Manning had a briefcase and a cassette tape recorder strapped over his shoulder. McCarter carried a portable typewriter in a metal case. Encizo held a miniature movie camera, and Ohara had a large aluminum valise and a Minolta 35mm camera, which dangled from a neck strap.

"What are you suppose to be?" Katz inquired. "A team of TV reporters?"

"That would have required forged identifications and phony passports," Encizo answered. "We're claiming to be contract personnel for a small independent film company that's planning a documentary on the Middle East."

"Our cover story allowed us to get some equipment through customs in Canada," Ohara said.

"Not much," McCarter shrugged. "But we did the best we could on short notice."

"We'll be able to get everything else we'll need," Katz assured them. "Let's pick up the rest of your luggage. Mossad has arranged for you to bypass the usual customs check. We don't have time to waste with such nonsense. We've got one hell of a job to take care of, my friends."

Ten minutes later, the five men of Phoenix Force emerged from the airport station and walked to a parking lot. Katz led them to a gray limousine parked in a reserved space.

"Nice car," Encizo remarked. "Who lent it to you?"

"Mossad, of course," Katz replied as he fished the car keys from his pocket. "I haven't had a chance to check it for listening devices."

"You think Mossad planted any in the car?" Manning asked.

"I'd be surprised if they haven't."

"I have a radio-frequency detector in my suitcase," Keio Ohara offered. "I can assemble it and sweep the vehicle for bugs if you think that's necessary."

"Sweep the car," Katz instructed.

"Allah akbar," a voice called out.

The men of Phoenix Force turned toward the sound. Two men were crouched behind a parked sedan. They braced their AK-47 assault rifles across the hood of the car, pointed the weapons at the five antiterrorists and opened fire.

5

Phoenix Force dived to the pavement the instant they saw the ambush. Twin volleys of full-auto fire scorched air above their heads. Bullets smashed into the metal skin of the limo. Glass shattered as 7.62mm rounds hit the windows.

Yakov Katzenelenbogen rolled onto his back and yanked the Beretta from his shoulder leather. He braced the pistol across his prosthetic arm and aimed at the ambushers. He was surprised to see both gunmen advancing from the shelter of the sedan. The idiots, assuming none of their victims were armed, had left themselves open.

"They're too stupid to live," Katz growled as he triggered the Beretta.

Two .380 hollowpoint slugs tore into the chest of the closest terrorist. The man fell against the side of the sedan and pulled the trigger of his Russian-made assault rifle. A burst of slugs chewed the pavement. Three bullets ricocheted back into the gunman, striking his lower torso. The terrorist collapsed on his belly, twitching feebly as death claimed his soul.

The second gunman kept coming, determined

to exterminate Phoenix Force. Before he could fire, Manning hurled his briefcase. The valise slammed into the terrorist's chest. The blow startled the killer who staggered backward, nearly tripping over the corpse of his former partner.

Katz thrust his Beretta at the terrorist, but David McCarter had already launched himself at the man. The Briton had responded to the opportunity to attack an enemy the way a greyhound reacts to a running rabbit. He crashed into the killer and both men toppled across the hood of the sedan.

Another burst of automatic fire suddenly smashed into the opposite side of the limousine. More glass exploded and bullets punched into the frame of the big car.

"The bastards have us surrounded," Manning muttered, prying the back plate from his cassette recorder.

"We need more firepower," Encizo said, trying to spot the positions of the new attackers.

The enemy was stationed behind more parked cars. Three terrorists lurked behind a Mercedes-Benz and at least two others were by a Jeep. Worse news was on its way—another trio of killers was rushing to the aid of the man who was grappling with McCarter.

"If we can hold out for a few seconds," Manning said, his calm tone concealing tension. "I can give them a hell of a surprise."

The Phoenix Force explosives expert had removed the back of his recorder and extracted a glob of white puttylike substance. He reached into his jacket and removed a large fountain pen. Unscrewing it in the middle, he unsheathed a pencil detonator with a timing dial one end.

"We'll see about buying you some time," Encizo replied.

The Cuban and Keio Ohara bolted from the limo. Katz fired his Beretta at the terrorists by the Mercedes, who were trying to blast Phoenix Force with two Russian PPSh-41 machine guns and an Israeli Uzi. Yakov realized he was hopelessly outgunned by his opponents, yet the ambushers were terrible marksmen, clearly unaccustomed to handling full-auto weapons.

Rafael Encizo scrambled to the discarded AK-47 that belonged to the terrorist Katz had killed. He gathered up the gun and quickly frisked the dead man, finding a spare magazine for the weapon.

David McCarter had managed to wrench the rifle from his opponent's grasp. When the AK-47 clattered on the ground, the terrorist attempted to grab McCarter's throat. The Briton blocked the man's groping hands with his forearms and promptly rammed a knee into his groin.

The terrorist doubled up in agony. McCarter quickly wrapped his left arm around the aggressor's neck to form a headlock and slammed his right fist into the man's face. The terrorist suffered two furious blows to the mouth and nose before he managed to extend an arm in an attempt to claw at McCarter's eyes. The Briton was familiar with such tactics. He twisted his face away from the gouging fingers and drove the top of the terrorist's head into the steel frame of the sedan.

The dazed man sagged in McCarter's grasp. The Englishman's left arm remained locked around the terrorist's throat as he pressed his right forearm against the base of the killer's skull. He grasped his own right elbow and left biceps to secure the hold. Then he dropped to one knee and increased pressure around the man's neck.

The forearm vise crushed the terrorist's windpipe, and his body convulsed in McCarter's lethal embrace. The stench of urine told the Briton his victim had lost control of his bodily functions. McCarter held on a moment longer to be certain the man was dead. He released the lifeless terrorist and scrambled to the dead man's AK-47.

The three Arab killers who had intended to rescue their comrade saw they were too late. They aimed their weapons at McCarter and prepared to open fire. Then a storm with flashing hands and feet suddenly fell upon them.

Keio Ohara dived feet first into the trio. One killer caught a glimpse of a blurred shape rushing toward his head. He turned sharply and received the bottom of Ohara's foot in his face. Shattered teeth popped from the man's mouth as he fell unconscious.

Ohara landed nimbly on his feet and kept

moving. The two remaining terrorists tried to swing their rifles toward the Japanese warrior. Ohara grabbed the closest man's AK-47 by the the barrel and yanked the killer off balance, shoving him into his partner.

Ohara hit the terrorist in the solar plexus with a karate *seiken* punch. The goon was still gasping from the first blow when Ohara's hand shot out again. He stabbed the tempered tips of his stiff fingers into the man's throat. The *nukite* stroke mashed the terrorist's Adam's apple into mush. He wilted to the ground and died.

The last of the terrorist trio was too close to Ohara to try to shoot him with the long-barreled AK-47. He desperately slashed a wild butt stroke at the Phoenix Force defender's head. Ohara weaved out of the path of the attack and snap-kicked his opponent in the gut. The thug folded at the waist. Ohara chopped the side of his hand across the back of the man's skull.

The terrorist fell to all fours. Keio Ohara screamed a fierce *kiai* and executed a deadly *empi* stroke. His elbow struck the fallen terrorist on the base of the neck, breaking the fragile seventh vertebrae and snapping the spinal cord with a single blow.

"These guys are nuts," Rafael Encizo said as he watched two terrorists bolt from the cover of the Jeep.

The pair boldly charged at the limo, one running to the front of the car, the other toward the back. Encizo pointed the AK-47 at the latter and squeezed the trigger. A 3-round burst of 7.62mm slugs punched through the terrorist's chest. The impact of the bullets kicked the zealot's body backward. He crashed into the Jeep and dropped face first to the ground.

Katz fired two .380 rounds into the other terrorist's upper torso. The Arab spun like a clumsy top, his gun flying from his grasp. But he did not fall. The man turned to again face Katz and drew a dagger from a belt sheath. He kept coming. Katz aimed the Beretta carefully and squeezed the trigger.

Nothing happened.

A bent cartridge casing jutted from the breech of the pistol. The terrorist shouted a victory cry when he realized Katz's Beretta had jammed. He scrambled onto the hood of the car, blood dripping from his bullet-torn chest. The man's eyes were ablaze with maniacal joy as he raised the knife.

Colonel Katzenelenbogen did not back away from the seemingly indestructible aggressor. He simply lowered the Beretta in his left fist, raised his right "hand" and pointed the index finger at the Arab.

Yellow flame burst from the end of his gloved finger. The terrorist heard the sharp crack of a high-velocity projectile breaking the speed of sound. A .22 Magnum slug smashed through the bridge of his nose. The Arab hardly felt the bullet slice through his brain, blasting out an exit hole the size of a dime in the back of his skull. He died too suddenly to realize what had happened.

The remaining terrorists were still stationed behind the Mercedes-Benz. They continued to fire at the Phoenix Force defenders. Bullets had destroyed the limousine: all four tires had been punctured and every window had been shattered.

Encizo fired his AK-47 at the gunmen's position. McCarter and Ohara, who had confiscated assault rifles from vanquished opponents, directed more salvos of bullets at the Mercedes. Despite the constant full-auto hail of metal slugs, only one window of the Mercedes had even been cracked.

"Son of a bitch," Encizo rasped. "That goddamn car is armor plated with reinforced bulletproof glass. Why didn't Mossad give us something like that instead of this cardboard limo?"

"They didn't think we'd need a tank disguised as a car," Katz replied. "I wonder if the owner of that Mercedes would like to sell it."

"Don't buy that car," Manning instructed as he pulled off his right shoe. "In another minute or two, it'll only be good for scrap metal."

"Cristo," Encizo hissed through clenched teeth when he saw a pool of liquid foaming under the belly of the limousine. "The gas tank has been punctured. If those bastards fire at the pavement, one spark could ignite the gasoline and blow us all to Valhalla."

"I remember what those Irish terrorists did in Seattle," Katz said tensely. "We have to move from this position fast. Spread out. We'll try to move in from both sides and get the enemy in a cross fire.''

''No need for that,'' Manning declared as he waved his shoe at the others.

''You're going to throw that at them?'' Encizo said, rolling his eyes.

''Trust me,'' Manning said.

The Canadian lobbed the shoe across the parking lot. It landed in front of the Mercedes.

The killers instantly ducked. One cried out in alarm. Then they recognized the object and burst into laughter. The terrorists aimed their weapons at the limo and prepared to open fire once more.

An explosion tore the Mercedes-Benz apart. Chunks of metal sailed into the sky. Thick plates of bullet-proof glass became flying fragments. Flaming gasoline splashed across the pavement.

The bodies of the three terrorists were torn. Arms and legs were ripped from their sockets. The three corpses dropped into the fiery wreckage that had formerly been the Mercedes-Benz.

''The shoe contained a quarter pound of C-4 plastic explosives with a pencil detonator,'' Manning explained.

''Good work, Gary,'' Katz told him, as he pulled the glove from his right hand.

The prosthetic arm was a contraption of steel and cables. The index finger was a hollow gun barrel. Katz gripped the barrel and twisted it from the socket, removing the spent shell casing of a .22 Magnum cartridge. He removed a metal pillbox from his pocket, which contained five fresh rounds for the finger gun. The Israeli reloaded the device, while McCarter, Encizo and Ohara checked the parking lot to make certain all enemies had been taken care of.

"We found a live one, Yakov," McCarter declared as he and Ohara dragged an unconscious terrorist by his ankles.

"Did you check him for hide-out weapons?" the Israeli asked.

"Yes," Ohara replied, holding a dagger in his left fist. "I found this under his shirt. The blade is stained with some sort of chemical. Probably poison."

"Cyanide," Katz said. "The two men who tried to kill the prime minister were also armed with such knives."

"An assassination attempt?" Manning asked. "What the hell is going on, Yakov?"

"A powder keg is set to explode," Katz answered. "If it does, we might well see the beginning of World War Three."

6

The director of Mossad is one of Israel's most powerful men. Espionage and counterintelligence have always been vital to Israel—clandestine operations are often more important than battlefield victories.

During the struggle for Israel's independence, there had been many Jewish intelligence organizations in operation: the Haganah, the Sherut Yediot, better known as the Shai, Rekhesh and Mossad.

In 1948, the current director of Mossad was a member of the Palmach, a special-missions strike force for Haganah.

After the war of independence, the director became the commander of the Barok Unit, a fighting squad assigned to carry out missions in hostile territory against radical terrorist groups. His team had traveled to Algeria, Syria and Lebanon to take action against such terrorist outfits as Black September.

The team had identified and found the Black September mastermind responsible for the 1972 massacre of Israeli athletes at the Olympic Village in Munich. Six years after the slaughter,

Mohammed Hassan Salameh paid for his crime with his life. Salameh and his bodyguards were blown to bits by a car bomb in Beirut.

The success of this operation was considered a great victory for Mossad—especially since a previous attempt had ended tragically when an Israeli hit team killed an innocent man in Norway whom they had mistaken for Salameh. Zwicka Zamir promptly promoted the man who had coordinated the Salameh operation. That man was destined to become Zamir's successor.

The director of Mossad had considerable background in direct-action missions. Thus he had great respect for Colonel Katzenelenbogen, one of the few men who had more experience in this field than himself. Yet he was stunned when Katz contacted him directly and requested a personal audience.

Actually, Katz's request had been a blunt command to meet him at the Tel Aviv Zoo at Mikve Yizra'el Square. The director was more accustomed to giving orders than taking them. The colonel's behavior was unorthodox if not outrageous, however, he realized Katzenelenbogen must have a very good reason for his actions.

The director arrived at the zoo alone. He wandered along the walkways, passing animal cages. He headed for the reptile house.

"Mister Director?" a voice whispered in Hebrew.

He turned to face the speaker. To his surprise he saw a middle-aged man dressed in an

abayeh—robe—and a *keffiyeh* around his head.
The director stiffened. Being involved in any intelligence organization causes a certain amount
of paranoia. The head of Mossad was especially
suspicious of Arabs.

"I am Katzenelenbogen," the stranger declared.

The director stared at the "Arab." He recognized the man's face from the personnel file on
Katzenelenbogen he had studied earlier.

"Please follow me, sir," Katz said as he led
the Mossad boss to a nearby restroom.

Katz ignored the handwritten sign tacked to
the door stating that the restroom was closed for
repairs. He rapped on the door and waited for a
two-knock reply. Then he rapped once more.
The door opened. The director was surprised to
see five men waiting inside the men's room.

One of the men was an Arab who glared at the
director with hatred. Dried blood was caked
around his split lips, but there was no other sign
of physical abuse. His hands appeared to be
bound behind his back and two other men aimed
silencer-equipped pistols at the Arab.

"I'm sure you wonder what is going on," Katz
said as he closed the bolted the door.

"That's an understatement, Colonel," the
director replied.

Katz quickly introduced him to the other men
of Phoenix Force. He told the director about the
incident at the airport. The Mossad chief listened
quietly, a grim expression on his face. When

Katz finished his story, the director addressed Phoenix Force in fluent English.

"What happened after the gun battle?" he asked.

"Naturally the police and airport security arrived to investigate," Katz said. "I showed them my Mossad identification and told them everything would be taken care of. There wasn't much trouble getting them to let us handle the matter, although the owner of the Mercedes-Benz was rather upset that his car had been demolished. I assured him the government would pay for the automobile."

"How kind of you," the director said.

"I thought so," Katz said. "By the way, the Mercedes belonged to the vice-chairman of the National Religious Party."

"There will be some angry demands for explanations from the NRP about this," the director said.

He looked at the Arab terrorist Phoenix Force had captured. "Has he told you anything yet?"

"Not even his name," Katz stated. "According to his ID, he's Ali Aboussan, a corporal in the Egyptian army air corps."

"Another Egyptian. This matter looks even worse than we thought."

"Let's not condemn Cairo too quickly," Katz urged. "Besides, we have another problem to deal with. It's the reason I had to see you personally. Someone in Israeli intelligence is in league with the terrorists."

"That's absurd. . . ."

"Then how do you explain the ambush that was waiting for us in the parking lot?" Manning inquired.

"The Arabs must have followed Colonel Katzenelenbogen."

"I think I would have spotted a tail," Katz said. "But even if the terrorists did follow me, they had to have a reason to do so in the first place."

"I can't believe anyone in Mossad would betray Israel," the director said. "You know how carefully we scan for loyalty in our people, Colonel."

"Traitors, defectors and sleeper agents can be found anywhere in the world," Manning said. "Why not in Israel?"

"Only three men knew I was going to be at the airport," Katz declared. "Major Eytan, Lieutenant Colonel Zavarj and Deputy Director Geller."

"You're suspicious of my second-in-command?" The Mossad director stared at the men of Phoenix Force as if he thought they had all escaped from an insane asylum.

"Trusting people isn't part of our job," McCarter stated in a hard flat voice. "Are you going to let us do our bloody job or are we going to piss around here all day arguing about the bleedin' infallibility of your organization?"

"What do you five have in mind?"

"We'll need a safehouse that isn't directly connected with Mossad or the Sheruth Modiin," Katz began. "And we'll need weapons."

The director glanced at the pistols McCarter

and Encizo used to cover the Arab prisoner. The Cuban held a compact, double-action Walther PPK, while the Briton had a considerably larger Browning Hi-Power. Both weapons had nine-inch sound suppressors attached to the muzzles.

"Where'd they get those guns?"

"We smuggled them into the country," McCarter replied. "You know how this sort of thing is done. The guns were disassembled and the parts placed into special compartments of large metal objects among our luggage. Metal detectors don't register anything unusual and X rays don't spot any suspicious shapes when there's that much metal all jammed together."

The director nodded. "We can supply you with any other weapons you might need. The selection includes American, British, German and South African guns as well as Israeli-made weapons."

"We might also need a translator," Manning said. "If we're forced to split up, Katz is the only member of the team who speaks both Hebrew and Arabic fluently. I learned a smattering of Arabic when I was in Egypt about twelve years ago, but I'll be damned if I remember more than a handful of words."

"Many Israelis speak English," the director said. "But I'll see to a translator in case you need one."

"And we'll have to get a competent medical team to interrogate the prisoner," Katz said.

"We have to get him to talk," Ohara stated as

he held up a pack of Egyptian cigarettes called Rames Special. "We found this in the terrorist's pocket. The cigarettes smell of prussic acid. Cyanide."

"It's a suicide device," McCarter said. "This bloke is a first-class fanatic. He won't break under conventional interrogation. Even torture might not work."

"All right," the director said, "bring him along...."

"Allah akbar," the Arab screamed as he started wildly twisting and turning.

His wrists had been bound behind his back with riot cuffs—a single strip of superstrong plastic. Regular handcuffs can be broken at the chain links by a desperate man with maniacal strength, but riot cuffs will not break; they must be clipped off with bolt cutters.

Everyone was astonished when the prisoner's arms suddenly swung free.

Blood jetted from the stump of the Arab's right arm. The fanatic had freed himself by literally ripping his own hand off at the wrist. The wrist joint had been torn apart by tugging and by violent wrenching; strands of muscle tissue hung from the stump.

Encizo gasped as the terrorist launched himself at the Cuban.

The Arab's left hand grabbed Encizo's fist that held the Walther PPK. The Cuban did not want to kill the captive. The guy would be punished enough by his own people for the rest of his life: the left hand is "unclean" in the Arab world and therefore not to be used, and a one-handed man is marked as a thief. The man still held on to Encizo's wrist. Suddenly he jammed the bleeding stump of his right arm into the Cuban's face.

McCarter rapidly closed in and slammed the frame of his Browning against the terrorist's skull. The madman's head was violently rocked to the side by the blow. He still refused to release Encizo.

The other members of Phoenix Force rushed forward to help subdue the lunatic. Then the report of a muffled gunshot sounded. The Arab staggered away from Encizo. A scarlet stain appeared in the center of his shirt. He tilted his head back and smiled. The smile remained after his bullet-punctured heart stopped and he fell to the floor dead.

"Damnation!" Encizo rasped. "The goddamn psycho pressed his chest into the muzzle and squeezed my finger around the trigger until the pistol went off."

"So much for questioning the prisoner," the Mossad director said.

"Jesus," Gary Manning said, glancing down at the severed hand. "He tore it off like a crazed animal caught in a steel trap. What kind of terrorists are we up against?"

"You already described them," Encizo replied as he unscrewed the silencer from the barrel of his Walther PPK. "Crazed animals."

7

The five men of Phoenix Force drove in the blue sedan along Petah Tikua Jabotinsky to the Diamond Exchange Center. The area was a hive of activity. Jewelers, diamond merchants and free-lance miners from at least a dozen countries discussed business transactions in almost as many different languages.

The scene looked bizarre to the four members of Phoenix Force who had never seen the Diamond Exchange before—Sephardic rabbis, dressed in their traditional black suits and hats, mingled with Saudi Arabians clad in *keffiyeh* and Savile Row suits. Germans, Greeks, South Africans and Japanese dealers in precious gems sat at sidewalk cafés and chatted about current trends in the international diamond-exchange market.

"I see it," Encizo quipped, "but I'm not sure I believe it."

"What you see is a group of diamond merchants," Katz explained. "Some are rabbis, some are Jesuit priests and the Arabs with the green *akal* on their *keffiyeh* are Muslims who have been to Mecca for the Holy Pilgrimage. Yet the hajjis get along with the other religious groups and vice versa because they're all diamond merchants. Maybe there's a key to world peace here, eh?''

"This is all quite interesting, Katz," McCarter said. "But what does this have to do with our mission?"

"I've got a friend in this district," the Israeli answered as he steered the sedan onto Derekh Abba Hillel. "He can arrange a safehouse for us."

"What about the one Mossad is going to supply us with?" Encizo asked.

"We can't consider it secure," Katz replied. "I want Mossad to *think* we'll set up at their safehouse. They won't know about the real one."

"You don't trust your own people?" Manning asked.

"You guys are my people," Katz stated. "As for Mossad, let's just say I trust them less than they trust us."

The sedan had been supplied by Mossad. It was an excellent car with armor plating, bulletproof glass and a sophisticated radio that could be used to receive or transmit to the director's office at the institute headquarters. However, when Ohara swept the vehicle with his radio detector, he found four wireless microphones that Mossad had planted in the car.

"You can't fault them for bugging the car," McCarter said. "We would have done the same in their place."

And when the car was made safe, Manning said, "I think it's time we talked about this mission, Katz."

"You want to know if Brognola ordered this action?" the Israeli asked. "The answer is no."

"So we're really on our own this time, aren't we?" McCarter said. The adventure-loving Briton sounded delighted with the idea. "Stony Man doesn't even know we're here and we can't trust Mossad."

"Yeah, that's just great," Manning muttered. Clearly he did not share McCarter's enthusiasm for an unauthorized and highly risky mission. "Bolan has fallen out of favor and has turned renegade. Stony Man is probably on the edge and the federal government might cancel the entire operation if they find out we're over here trying to take on the whole Middle East single-handed."

"Not a good time to make waves," Encizo added. "We're really in a mess."

"Phoenix Force is suppose to fight terrorism," Ohara remarked. "Isn't our duty more important than who orders us to the task?"

"Bloody right," McCarter agreed. "We've got a job to do. That's what matters."

"I wouldn't have involved Phoenix Force in this if the situation wasn't critical," Katz told his teammates. "But what other choice is there? Israeli intelligence thinks the Egyptian government is responsible for the assassination attempt on the prime minister. This could easily lead to violence. The Middle East can't stand any more hostilities. I doubt that the president of the United States would be happy to see everything that was accomplished by the Camp David peace talks go down the drain.''

''Not to mention the high probability of a war in the Middle East,'' Ohara added.

''Well,'' Encizo began, ''I'll tell you one thing's for sure—those terrorists are going to try again. They wouldn't have attacked us at the airport unless they wanted us out of the way so they could take another crack at the prime minister.''

''I agree, Rafael,'' Katz said. ''And if the terrorists do assassinate the prime minister and succeed in framing Egypt for the killing, Israel *will* retaliate.''

''You think Israel would attack Egypt?'' Manning asked.

''The government is comprised of a large number of hard-line hawks,'' Katz replied. ''Most of them saw what happened in Europe in the 1940s. Most of them believe Israel has to be tough in order to survive.

''If Israel launches an attack against Egypt,'' Katz continued, ''it would probably ruin any hope of ever having peaceful negotiation with the Arab world in the future. Some of the rabble-rousers would probably even claim the Israelis assassinated their prime minister simply to have an excuse to break the treaty with Egypt. It would certainly result in more violence and bloodshed.''

''And war,'' Manning added. ''Israel has gotten a lot of bad press lately. The United Nations has condemned the country's actions in Lebanon and even the United States has been critical of Israel from time to time. The Arabs might see this as an ideal chance to band together and attack Israel in unison.''

"Syria and Libya would probably agree to that," McCarter remarked. "Jordan might join the movement—unless they're too busy with another conflict."

"The United States would come to Israel's aid," Encizo stated. "The terrorists are wrong if they think otherwise."

"And the Soviets would back the hostile Arabs," Manning added. "Whether the Arabs wanted the Russian Bear on their side or not."

"And you can bet your arse somebody would start firing nuclear missiles before long," McCarter stated.

"Any of you read the Bible?" Manning asked.

The question surprised his teammates. Encizo shrugged. "Not for a long time," he admitted.

"I just thought of a passage from the Book of Revelations," the Canadian said. "It concerns the final battle before the end of the world. 'And he gathered them together into a place called in the Hebrew tongue Armageddon.' "

"Well," McCarter quipped, grinning. "I didn't find any place called Armageddon in the ruddy tourist guide."

"Colonel Katzenelenbogen," a voice called from the car radio.

Yakov had removed the stiff, five-fingered prosthetic device in favor of a three-prong hook that resembled an eagle's talon. Katz gathered up the microphone from the radio with his hook and pressed a button.

"Katz here."

"When can you and your men return to headquarters?" the Mossad director asked.

"Something urgent?"

"I think you'll find it of interest," the director answered. "You may also like to talk to a couple visitors from Egypt."

Katz raised his eyebrows. "Indeed. We'll be there as soon as possible."

Katz turned the sedan around in a driveway and headed back toward the Institute of Intelligence and Special Missions. Driving down Hanitsahon Street, Phoenix Force approached a construction site where an apartment complex was being built. A large dump truck suddenly backed onto the road, blocking the sedan.

"Trouble?" McCarter asked as he reached for a briefcase by his feet.

"Maybe," Katz said. He applied the brakes and slowed to a stop.

Encizo, seated next to Katz, snapped open a suitcase containing two Uzi submachine guns with folding wire stocks. Mossad had supplied Phoenix Force with the hardware, and the team had already tested the weapons at an indoor firing range.

Gary Manning unzipped a leather rifle case

and extracted an American-made M-16 assault rifle with an M-203 grenade launcher attached to the barrel. Keio Ohara reached inside his jacket for a U.S. Government Issue 1911A1 pistol.

Three Arab gunmen popped out from inside the body of the truck. Their heads, shoulders and machine guns jutted over the side. They took aim at the sedan. Automatic weapons opened fire.

Bullets whined off the thick plates of shatter-proof glass in the windshield. The five men inside the car automatically ducked, although none of the projectiles broke through the reinforced glass barrier.

"Trouble," McCarter muttered as he yanked an Ingram M-10 out of the briefcase.

Katz shifted gears into reverse and stomped on the gas. The sedan shot backward, tires screeching. Yakov glanced in the rearview mirror as more machine-gun rounds slammed into the windshield and hood.

A truck with a cement mixer attached rolled onto the road behind the sedan. Katz spun the steering wheel to avoid the new obstacle. More machine-gun-toting Arabs appeared from both sides of the cement mixer. They started blasting the sedan with automatic lead.

Not even bullet-proof glass could withstand continued bombardment from high-velocity projectiles for long. Cracks appeared in the windshield and side windows as Katz drove backward over the curb.

David McCarter opened a door and jumped

outside. Using the body of the sedan for cover, he aimed the Ingram at the terrorists closing in on foot. The Briton had chosen the M-10 from the Mossad arms selection because it was his favorite close-quarters automatic weapon. A boxlike gun with a stubby barrel and a short wire stock, the Ingram did not look very formidable, but it was dependable, sturdy and featured a 32-round capacity.

The Englishman triggered his M-10 and blasted a 3-round burst into the chest of the closest Arab. The terrorist was knocked off his feet and sent tumbling to the ground in a dying heap. Another killer kept advancing. McCarter hit him with a diagonal volley of 9mm slugs that opened him up from hip to breastbone.

As the second terrorist fell, Keio Ohara and Rafael Encizo emerged from the car. The Cuban sprayed the dump truck with Uzi rounds. One Arab's head exploded like a blood-filled balloon. The others dropped behind the frame of the truck bed.

Ohara braced his arms across the hood of the sedan, the big Colt automatic held in a two-handed weaver combat grip. He aimed the gun at the chest of another charging Arab and squeezed the trigger. A 185-grain hollowpoint slug punched into the center of the terrorist's chest. The impact of the heavy .45-caliber bullet kicked the man back against the side of the cement mixer.

Katz and Manning climbed out of the sedan. The Israeli chopped down two advancing Arab terrorists with a slashing volley of 9mm slugs. Bullets smashed into throats and faces, nearly decapitating the pair. Holding the Uzi braced across his artificial arm, Katz joined Ohara and McCarter at the front of the car.

"There are more of the bastards on the opposite side of the cement mixer," the Briton declared.

"Wait until Rafael and Gary open fire on the enemy stationed at the dump truck," Katz told McCarter. "We want those bastards to be preoccupied before we make our move."

"*Allah akbar*. . . ." an Arab cried as he charged forward. He ran right into a well-placed .45 bullet that Ohara drilled into his heart.

"Keio," Katz said, "you and David prepare to rush the cement mixer. I'll supply cover fire to keep the enemy pinned down."

The Japanese nodded.

The driver of the dump truck shifted gears and pulled his vehicle forward, attempting to attain a better angle, allowing his comrades to get a clear target. Encizo trained his Uzi on the cab and opened fire.

Nine-millimeter projectiles dissolved glass and blasted the driver's skull into a bloodied pulp. He slumped behind the steering wheel. Gary Manning triggered a salvo of 5.56mm rounds at the terrorists inside the body of the dump truck.

The Arabs ducked and bullets ricocheted off the truck's frame. Manning braced his M-16 against a hip and raised the barrel to judge the distance between himself and the dump truck. Satisfied, he reached under the barrel of the M-203 sleeve attachment and fired the grenade launcher.

A 40mm projectile full of heavy explosives sailed into the belly of the dump truck. The high-explosive round blasted apart the big metal container. The heavy steel walls broke loose and fell to earth along with the shredded, gory remains of the two terrorists.

"Now," Katz shouted.

He swung his Uzi toward the cement mixer and fired a long burst at the enemy, hosing the area with 9mm rounds. Terrorists scrambled behind the big vehicle for cover. One lunatic attacked, waving his AK-47 overhead as if wielding a scimitar instead of a gun. Katz blasted him with the last four rounds from the Uzi magazine. The man stumbled, landed on his knees and dropped his rifle. He opened his mouth, vomited a tide of crimson and fell dead on his face.

Ohara and McCarter bolted from cover and ran to the back of the cement truck. The Japanese threw himself to the ground, landing on his side with the .45 aimed at the startled terrorists at the side of the truck.

The Colt roared, burning a bullet into the lower intestines of one of the four Arabs lurking by the mixer. The man doubled up in agony. Ohara ignored him for the moment and fired another .45 slug into the upper torso of a terrorist who was about to swing a Russian sub gun toward the Japanese warrior.

McCarter poked the Ingram around the edge of the cement mixer and sprayed the remaining pair of terrorists with a lethal hail of 115-grain projectiles. An Arab's face vanished. The other man was spun around by the 9mm rounds that crashed into his chest and shoulder. He turned in time to receive two more bullets in the base of the neck, severing his spinal cord.

The man who Ohara had gut-shot tried to gather up his Kalashnikov for another attempt to kill the infidels. Ohara's 1911A1 snarled once more. A .45 slug crashed through the man's forehead. The back of his head exploded.

"Are you two all right?" Katz asked as he jogged forward to join Ohara and McCarter.

"Ducky," the Briton answered. "Couldn't get any of these blokes alive. From the sound of that explosion, I guess Gary and Rafael didn't manage to take any prisoners, either."

"No," Katz confirmed. "Instead we've got about a dozen more dead bodies and no answers. At least we're alive."

"Might not be so easy to stay that way if things like this keep happening," McCarter commented.

8

Twenty minutes later, Phoenix Force was introduced to two Egyptian Security Force's agents.
Major Nizam and Captain Malik were waiting
for them in the Mossad director's office.

"It took you men quite a while to get here,"
the director remarked.

"We were delayed by traffic," Katz replied.
"I'll explain later. Why did Cairo send you two
gentlemen?" he asked the Egyptians.

"We were sent by our government because
we've learned that Mossad believes the Arab Republic of Egypt was involved in an attempt to
assassinate your prime minister," Nizam explained. He was a tall, waspy man with a
hawkish nose and coal-black eyes. "We want to
help you find out who is really responsible."

"How did you learn about the assassination
attempt?" the Mossad boss asked.

"We have intelligence sources within Israel,"
Captain Malik, a muscular young Arab, replied.
"Please do not ask us to reveal them. You would
only force us to lie to you."

"But you wouldn't lie to us about a scheme to
kill the prime minister?" the director snorted. He

turned to Katz. "Well, Colonel. Do you trust them?"

"At this point I'm not ready to trust anyone except my four partners," Yakov answered bluntly. "But I don't think the Egyptian government is responsible for the attempt on the prime minister's life—or the two attempts to try to kill my teammates and myself."

"*Two* attempts?" the director said, raising his eyebrows.

"The second happened on our way over here," Encizo said coldly. "Right after *you* called us on the radio."

"You're saying you suspect I set you up?" the Mossad chief snapped.

"Not at all," Manning assured him. "In fact, the style of the attack proves you can be trusted."

"The bastards opened fire on us with machine guns," McCarter explained. "If they'd known we had an armor-plated car with bullet-proof glass, they would have used grenades or a bomb planted in the middle of the road."

"However," Keio Ohara said, "we suggest you change the frequency of your radio communications. They're obviously not secure."

"I'm glad Colonel Katzenelenbogen believes my government isn't involved in this sordid business," Nizam remarked. "Of course, we understand any doubts you people have about our intentions. We want to offer to assist you in any way to earn your trust."

"You might start by getting whatever information you can concerning the Egyptians who have been involved in these terrorist actions," Katz told him.

"Give me the names and we'll contact Cairo," Nizam assured him. "Within twelve hours we'll have complete files on the men involved."

"Mossad has been trying to identify the men your group killed this morning," the director said.

"What have you found so far?" Encizo asked.

"At least three were Egyptians, two others are from the Arab Quarter here in Tel Aviv," the director answered. "We're still working on the rest. There may never be a positive ID on the men who were blown to bits."

"Do you have the former addresses of the two Israeli Arabs?" Encizo asked.

"Of course. Do you think you'll find anything of value there?"

"Might have a look and find out," McCarter commented.

"How about the security for the prime minister?" Manning asked. "The terrorists will try again. We'd better be ready for them when they do."

"We've tightened security," the director said. "Only a handful of people know where he really is. Very few have known from the start. That's why the assassins shot up a department-store dummy when they made their first attempt to kill him."

"Mind if we see if there are any improvements that your people may have overlooked?" the Canadian asked.

"Of course not," the Mossad man said, but his tone revealed that the suggestion offended him.

"Have autopsies been performed on the dead terrorists?" Katz inquired.

"That's currently in progress," the director said. "Apparently, that will take even longer since we'll have some more bodies now. How many terrorists did you kill on your way here?"

"About a dozen," Katz shrugged.

"Since we already know why the men were killed, we are more concerned with identifying them at this time," the Mossad chief stated. "There doesn't seem to be any other reason to hurry the autopsies."

"I disagree," Katz told him. "Those terrorists were absolutely fearless. You saw how our prisoner ripped off his own hand to commit suicide. That's incredibly fanatical behavior even for a terrorist."

"You think they may have some sort of drug in their blood?" Ohara asked.

"I wouldn't be surprised," Katz answered. "Morphine addicts have been known to be crazy brave and totally immune to pain. PCP junkies have also been known to have superhuman strength. Some have gone beserk and attacked police officers who have emptied a service revolver into a PCP freak without stopping him."

"Do you want to check with Dr. Ben-David in our medical department?" the director asked.

"Yes. I'd also like to examine the bodies personally."

"The bodies?" Nizam said, raising his eyebrows. "Are you looking for anything in particular, Colonel?"

"One never knows where information is stored," Katz replied. "Sometimes a dead man can tell you quite a bit."

"Oh, I selected a translator for your group," the director stated. "Lieutenant Stern has been working in linguistics for more than ten years, first in the army and later with Mossad. Speaks Hebrew, Arabic, English and French fluently. Highly reliable. Good background."

"Sounds like he'll do," McCarter said.

"She," the director said, smiling. "Lieutenant *Rachel* Stern."

9

Rafael Encizo found Rachel Stern to be far more interesting than the scenery they were passing.

She was a beautiful woman in her late twenties. She had raven-black hair, a tan complexion and bright green eyes. Driving the Toyota Land Rover with expertise, she was wearing a short-sleeved white blouse and a khaki skirt.

But, while Rafael was taken in by the translator, she paid little attention to his attempts to strike up a casual conversation.

David McCarter, who was riding in the back of the Jeep, did not even bother to try and chat with Rachel. He had labeled her as a cold customer as soon as they had been introduced. She seemed to bristle with resentment when she heard his British accent.

The Englishman intended to concentrate on the job. If his Cuban partner wanted to try to charm the chip off her shoulder, that was his business—as long as Encizo's romantic notions did not get in the way of their mission.

Rachel parked the Jeep beside a curb on Yefet Street in front of an apartment building and turned off the engine.

"This is the address," she announced.

"Both of the Israeli Arab terrorists had apartments in this building?" Encizo asked.

"Yes," Rachel said, slipping the strap of a large purse over her shoulder. "The landlord may not be very pleased to have a trio of 'infidels' checking on his former tenants, but he'll cooperate with Mossad if he wants to stay in business."

Her prediction proved accurate. The landlord was displeased by their demands to search the rooms of the recently departed Mohammed Bashir and Abu Hammad. He reluctantly surrendered a key and gave Rachel the room numbers and directions to them.

The woman led McCarter and Encizo up a flight of stairs to the second floor where they found Hammad's room. She unlocked the door and they entered. The apartment was a mess with dirty clothes and old newspapers scattered across the floor. Unwashed plates and teacups were piled on a battered table, and the stuffing bulged from a rip in the mattress on Hammad's bed. In contrast, a clean rug lay on the center of the wooden floor with an area neatly swept around it.

"A prayer rug," Rachel explained. "A devoted Muslim prays three times a day, facing Mecca."

McCarter, searching the apartment, found a banana-shaped magazine for an AK-47 in one of the drawers.

"I found a map with Ben Gurion airport circled in red," Encizo announced as he rummaged through a cabinet under the sink. "And a small bottle of liquid which smells like prussic acid."

"Who ever heard of bloody terrorists in the twentieth century using poison daggers?" the Englishman muttered. McCarter than looked at Rachel who was giving him a cold stare. "What in piss is buggin' you?"

"I'm afraid we Israelis don't find you British to be such charming characters," Rachel remarked stiffly as she knelt by a steamer trunk. "Since we had to fight England for our independence."

"So did the Yanks and they don't seem to hold a grudge," McCarter shrugged. "Lighten up."

"Maybe when two hundred years have passed we won't hold a grudge either," she told him.

"Well, the British could still be pissed with the fact the Zionists blew up the King David Hotel and killed a lot of innocent people," the Englishman stated. "They also executed a lot of British soldiers without bothering with a trial. Yet England has been willing to bury the hatchet and be an ally to Israel. Why can't you accept that, Lieutenant Stern?"

"If you two can give this conversation a rest," Encizo announced, "you might take a look at this."

The Cuban showed them a metal bottle with a ceramic cup fixed to the neck and a long hoselike stem attached to the base. McCarter took the water pipe and sniffed its bowl.

"Hashish," he remarked. "A lot of terrorists use drugs of one kind or another. They're not really professional soldiers or espionage agents. Even the bastards who receive professional training aren't prepared for the stress, fear and boredom that's part of the trade."

"Okay," Encizo said, handing him a metal amulet with a crude symbol engraved on it. "How about this?"

"Some sort of mystical nonsense," the Englishman stated. "Doesn't look like any Islamic symbol I'm familiar with. What do you say, Lieutenant?"

"I don't recognize it either," she admitted as she checked inside the steamer trunk. "But look at this."

She held up a white *brussa* that had the same emblem on the left breast side. The two Phoenix Force warriors examined it.

"Think there's a connection here?" Encizo asked.

"Maybe," McCarter said. "Let's check the other chap's room."

The quarters of the late Mohammed Bashir proved that all terrorists were not slobs. The furniture was cheap, but well cared for. The floor had been recently swept. There was also a well-stocked bookcase, a floor lamp, a table, two wooden chairs and a wall locker that served as a clothes closet.

"Rachel, take a look at those books," Encizo said. "See if there are any translations of the works of Marx, Lenin or Carlos Marighella."

"Who?" she asked.

"Marighella was an old comrade of Castro's," Encizo explained. "He wrote a manual on the principles of terrorism which has become sort of a bible for a lot of groups throughout the world. It's been translated into at least a dozen languages including Arabic."

McCarter opened the closet. "Bingo," he announced, extracting a white *brussa* on a wire hanger. "Same symbol on the shirt."

"Another pipe, too," Encizo declared as he searched through a cabinet.

"There's a copy of the Koran here," Rachel said as she knelt by the bookcase.

"Anything else?" Encizo asked.

"A volume of Islamic poetry, a book about the seven Imams who succeeded Mohammed and one about the Lord of All Ages."

"What's that?" McCarter asked. "Sounds like science fiction."

"I'm not sure," Rachel said. "But all of these appear to be devotional books. No Communist literature in the lot."

"Well," Encizo sighed. "I guess we'll...."

"Allah akbar," several voices cried in unison.

McCarter, Encizo and Rachel turned to see five knife-wielding Arabs charging into the room, their faces resembling wild beasts.

The terrorists attacked too swiftly for either Encizo or McCarter to draw a gun from shoulder leather.

Encizo quickly slammed a boot into the table,

sending it skidding into the path of three terrorists. The trio staggered away from the table while
the other two attacked.

The Cuban grabbed a chair and swung it into
the nearest opponent, blocking a knife thrust. He
shoved forcibly, driving two chair legs into
the terrorist's chest. The Arab stumbled and Encizo's leg lashed out, driving a foot into the man's
groin.

The terrorist grasped his damaged testicles in
one hand and fell to his knees. Encizo brought
the chair crashing down on his opponent's head,
cracking the Arab's skull. The Cuban saw the
blur of another attacker out of the corner of his
eye. He pivoted and slashed the chair into the
second terrorist before the man could strike with
his poison dagger.

Encizo swung the chair again, but the Arab
suddenly launched a powerful roundhouse kick
at the Phoenix fighter. The terrorist's boot
struck the chair hard, ripping it from Encizo's
grasp. The Cuban saw the next kick coming and
managed to avoid the Arab's slashing foot.

The Phoenix pro recognized the terrorist's
fighting style—*savate*, a form of French kick
boxing. The terrorist attempted a wild knife
slash, a feint followed by another kick aimed at
Encizo's groin.

The trick did not fool the Cuban. He dodged
the false dagger stroke and caught his opponent's
attacking leg at the ankle. Encizo twisted hard,
throwing the Arab off balance. The man tum-

bled to the floor. He screamed violently as he rolled into the nearest wall. The terrorist rose to his knees and stared at his own knife. It was lodged deeply in his chest. The fanatic slumped to the floor and died.

David McCarter had seized the floor lamp by its long metal stem. He swung the heavy brass base from the floor and thrust it into the stomach of a charging terrorist. The blow lifted the man off his feet and propelled him backward into another Arab killer.

Given a second to breathe, the Briton discarded the lamp and yanked his Browning Hi-Power from its shoulder holster. He snapped off the safety catch as two knife-wielding terrorists charged at him.

McCarter shot the closest attacker in the face. A 9mm hollowpoint slug split the bridge of the Arab's nose and sizzled through his brain, turning his skull into a gory mess.

The second terrorist pounced on McCarter. Only the Briton's combat-honed reflexes saved him from a poison-dagger thrust. The pair clutched wrists, negating the terrorist's knife and McCarter's Browning.

McCarter did not waste time. He stomped a boot heel into the terrorist's instep and butted his forehead into the other man's face. Before his startled adversary could recover, McCarter raised his arms and pivoted, pulling the Arab with him.

Standing back to back with the terrorist,

McCarter bent and hurled the startled Arab over his head. The man crashed to the floor, landing hard on his belly. There was no time to be sporting. McCarter promptly shot the scum in the back of the skull.

Rachel Stern opened her purse and reached for a .38 Smith & Wesson snub-nosed revolver as the last terrorist attacked. She sidestepped a knife thrust and kicked the side of the man's knee. His leg buckled, but he still managed to slash a backhand stroke at Rachel.

The pretty Israeli raised her purse to block the knife blade. Then she rammed a knee into the man's gut. He doubled up with a grunt, but the fanatical fury in his eyes warned he still had plenty of fight left.

Encizo stepped forward and delivered a solid uppercut to the Arab's jaw. He followed with a powerful left jab. The killer was driven backward by the impact of the punches.

The terrorist shook his head to try and clear it. Flecks of blood flew from his nose and mouth. With a snarl, he set himself to attack. McCarter swung his Browning at the fanatic. Rachel pulled the .38 revolver from her purse and Encizo drew his Walther PPK. All three opened fire. Bullets tore into the terrorist's chest and sent him hurtling across the room. His corpse hit the wall and slid to the floor in a lifeless heap.

"Well," McCarter said as he holstered his pistol. "I'd say we've found enough bloody proof to suggest we're on the right track."

10

Phoenix Force met in a conference room at Mossad Headquarters. Encizo and McCarter told the others about the incident at the Arab Quarter as Colonel Katzenelenbogen examined the *bruss*—shirts—and amulet.

"It's a symbol that looks vaguely familiar, but I'm not certain where I've seen it before," Katz said. "These terrorists certainly put a lot of stock in mystical symbols. We found a crude star-shaped tattoo on several of the dead terrorists. Most of the tattoos were located on the inner thigh or the hip. They weren't just decorations."

"Skin amulets?" Encizo said.

"Why not?" Yakov replied. "They could never misplace a tattoo as our departed friend did with this."

Katz tossed the brass amulet onto the table. McCarter glanced at it and shrugged. "Not much of a good-luck charm," he said. "Fellow's dead."

"Did you guys find anything else?" Gary Manning asked as he sipped a cup of black coffee.

"Not much," Encizo answered. "Both of the terrorists had hash pipes in their rooms."

"The autopsies revealed that all of the slain terrorists were using a great deal of drugs," Katz said. "Besides hashish, there were also traces of synthetic heroin and various types of uppers, downers."

"The two dead terrorists we checked out both appeared to be religious," Encizo added. "One guy had a bookcase full of Muslim literature. The Koran and some other books including one called the Master of the Ages."

"The Lord of All Ages?" Katz inquired.

"That's it," McCarter said. "Is it important?"

"Well, the Ismailis believe that the Lord of All Ages is a mystical representative of Allah," Katz explained. "The Ismailis are followers of Ismail, one of the seven Imams who succeeded Mohammed the Prophet. This gets a bit confusing because Ismail had a son who was also named Mohammed and the Lord of All Ages is suppose to be his mystical ally."

"Sort of like a Catholic saint?" Encizo inquired.

"More like a cross between a saint and the Pope," Katz corrected. "The Lord of All Ages is a living being on earth."

"Wait a minute," Manning said, "I've heard of the Ismailis. Isn't the Aga Khan associated with them?"

"That's right," McCarter declared. "And one

of the Aga Khan's ancestors was an ally to the British during the Afghan War. He was the head of a sect called the Khojas.''

''But there was another sect that started more than eight hundred years ago with a far more sinister reputation than the Khojas,'' Katz stated. ''The Hashishin—better known as the Assassins.''

''Assassins?'' Manning asked.

''The word assassin comes from Hashishin, which means ''drugger.'' The cult was started by a Persian named Hassan. Hassan made enemies of a sultan and a vizier, who managed to convince the Shah to expel Hassan from the country.

''While in exile,'' Yakov continued, ''Hassan formed the secret society in Egypt that came to be known as the Assassins. Raised as an Ismaili, Hassan was familiar with the mysticism associated with the religion. He had also been a student of the brilliant Imam Muwafig and trained in the Shia arts of influencing people. According to legend, Hassan got his first followers when he was on board a ship sailing to north Africa. During a bad storm, Hassan told the passengers and crew that he could change the weather and save them if they swore allegiance to him.''

''I would have told him to go to hell,'' McCarter said.

''Most of the people on the ship did exactly that,'' Katz confirmed. ''But after the storm ceased, two of the passengers believed Hassan had indeed displayed divine powers and they followed him off the vessel at the end of the journey.''

"How did Hassan build an organization like that from only two followers?" Ohara inquired.

"He attracted young Ismailis and convinced them he was a prophet of Allah," Katz answered. "He not only manipulated his followers verbally and with drugs, he actually took them to paradise as well.''

"What?" Encizo asked.

"Hassan found a beautiful tranquil valley near Cairo," Katz explained. "Hassan drugged his initiates and transported them to the valley, where they awoke surrounded by flowers and rivers of milk and wine. Beautiful women danced for them and provided sexual pleasures.''

"Sounds like Paradise to me," McCarter commented.

"That's why Hassan's followers believed they were in heaven," Katz said. "Naturally, they drugged the initiates again and returned them to Hassan. He told them they had seen paradise and the only way to achieve it for eternity was to follow his word.''

"Incredible," Manning remarked.

"Hassan's people followed his every command," Katz said. "They were totally fearless. In fact, they welcomed death. To die in the service of their prophet meant they would certainly go to paradise forever.

"Hassan knew how to use zealots," Katz continued. "He sent them out to infiltrate cities and palaces, disguised as merchants, priests and beggars. They formed a sophisticated intelligence network. Assassins even penetrated the courts of sultans and shieks, becoming trusted advisors to Arab royalty. Then Hassan took on clients who would pay handsomely to have certain individuals killed.''

"Who hired the Assassins?" Ohara asked.

"The crusaders were their biggest client," Katz answered. "The Europeans were getting the hell kicked out of them by the Islamic forces when they tried to lay claim to the Holy Land. So they hired the Assassins to kill Muslim rulers and generals.

"The Assassins were a fearsome power in the Middle East for more than two hundred years," the Israeli said. "And the organization extended across the entire Islamic empire. There were branches of the cult in Syria, India, Afghanistan and the Pamir Mountains, which border China and Russia."

"What happened to them?" Manning inquired.

"After Hassan's death," Katz said, "a series of successors followed as leaders of the secret society. None of them were as clever as the cult's founder. Bad management caused many mistakes. Sultan Saladin had dozens of Assassins killed in retaliation for an unsuccessful attempt on his life. The society was also spread too thin to keep the chain of command intact. It eventually broke up, but it never truly vanished."

"And you think we're dealing with the Assassins now?" Encizo asked. "That seems pretty farfetched, Katz."

"Someone has revised the Order of the Assassins," Katz declared. "Everything supports it. Poison daggers are the traditional weapon of the Assassins. The terrorists' behavior is identical to that of the Assassins of old."

"If you're correct about this," Manning began, "how could they infiltrate a Jewish intelligence organization like Mossad. Doesn't one have to be Jewish to join Mossad or the Sheruth Modiin?"

"That's correct," Katz confirmed. "But that doesn't mean they can't be infiltrated by non-Jewish agents. The Assassins had little in common with Sunni Muslims, yet they successfully infiltrated the palaces of sultans and caliphs. An Arab agent could easily pass as a Jew. It could be done. I'm convinced it has been done."

"I suggest we do a bit of research," Ohara said. "If the emblem on their shirts and the star tattoos are indeed Assassin symbols, it would confirm your theory."

"Good idea, Keio," the Israeli agreed. "How's the security for the prime minister?"

"Good," Manning answered. "He has plenty of protection, but any system can be beaten. Keio and I suggested that he be transferred from the Straus Health Centre to a military hospital in Nablus, but he refused."

"Did he give a reason?" Katz asked.

"The prime minister has pretty much recovered from the effects of the heart attack," the Canadian said. "The doctors still want him to rest for a while, but he intends to go back to work in a couple days."

"He'd probably be safer to just stay put," Encizo commented.

"Well," Manning gestured helplessly, "the worse news is the fact the prime minister wants to hold a press conference in the hospital rose garden tomorrow morning."

"Jesus," McCarter groaned. "He'll be a sitting target for the bastards."

"He seems to think the conference is important enough to take that risk," Manning said. "And the prime minister is a very stubborn man."

"I know," Katz said. "The prime minister is an old acquaintance. Perhaps I should talk to him."

"Good luck," the Canadian remarked.

"Well," McCarter sighed. "What next?"

"The terrorists obviously have a branch here in Tel Aviv," Katz said. "You and Rafael can continue to check that angle."

"The Tel Aviv police might be able to help," Encizo commented. "If they can tell us where to find any local dope dealers. We might be able to lean on a couple pushers to get some information about the terrorists' hashish connection. Could lead to bigger fish."

"Worth a try," Katz said.

"If it can wait until tomorrow," the Cuban said, "I'd like to see Rachel home."

"Girl chasing on the job?" Manning said, grinning. "That's not like you, Rafael."

"Girl chasing at any time is just like him," McCarter laughed.

"Just make certain you and Lieutenant Stern are back here by seven o'clock tomorrow morning," Katz said to Encizo with a wink.

11

"Are you a true believer, Ali?" Hassan asked the nervous youth who stood before the cult leader.

"I am, master," the boy replied. His voice was firm, but his body trembled as he spoke.

Ali was only fifteen years old, scrawny, illiterate and naive. He wore a pair of crudely patched trousers and a threadbare shirt, the only clothes he owned after selling all his worldly possessions to make an adequate contribution to the Order.

"Your faith is flawed, Ali," Hassan told the youth. "I can see that in your soul. You are not without fear of death."

"I believe in Allah, the one true God," Ali answered, hoping this would please Hassan.

"Your faith is weak, Ali," the cult leader sighed. "You speak of Allah, but you do not believe in Him strongly enough. You doubt my word and you doubt paradise in the next world."

"Master, I . . ." Ali began lamely.

"You shall lose your fear of death, weak one," Hassan stated. "You will discover the great truth. I shall send you to paradise."

Jemal, Hassan's manservant, stepped from behind his master's throne and raised his arm. He held an old .45-caliber Webley revolver. Ali's eyes bulged and his mouth fell open when he saw the gun pointed at his chest. Jemal squeezed the trigger.

The roar of the revolver filled the room. The orange muzzle-flash illuminated the horror-struck features of the youth as the bullet crashed into his flesh. Ali's feet left the carpeted floor. He fell heavily, a scarlet stain creeping across the front of his shirt.

"WHY DID YOU KILL THAT BOY?" Colonel Fawzi demanded when he met with Hassan an hour later in the cult leader's secret chambers.

"I see you've been watching the closed-circuit television again," Hassan remarked. "Are you really that bored here, Colonel?"

"Did you kill him just to impress your follow-ers with your godlike power over them?" Fawzi sneered.

"Really, Colonel," Hassan sighed. "How I operate my organization is not of your concern."

"It is if I have reason to believe you've gone totally mad," the terrorist colonel said bluntly. "You wouldn't be the first so-called prophet who began to believe his own propaganda."

"What an absurd accusation," Hassan chuck-led. "Very well. To ease your mind about my sanity, I'll explain what you saw."

Hassan strolled to his sofa and sprawled across it. "You did not witness an execution, Colonel."

"It looked like murder to me," Fawzi told him.

"Don't pretend to be a moralist, Colonel," Hassan smiled. "Your United Arab Front has been responsible for many murders in the past."

"That has nothing to do with what I saw today," Fawzi insisted. "Your slave killed that boy...."

"Your eyes deceived you, Colonel," Hassan said. "Things are not always as they seem. The boy was shot in the chest, but he is not dead."

"Please explain," Fawzi urged.

"The bullet was made of wax. It contained a powerful tranquilizer in liquid form, dyed red for effect. The force of the .45-caliber slug knocked the boy over and no doubt stunned and startled him. A tiny needle, no thicker than a strand of wire, was inside the wax to insure that enough of the drug would enter the boy's bloodstream through the puncture in his skin. The boy was merely sedated, although he appeared to have been killed right before the eyes of spectators, including yourself."

"Ingenius," Fawzi admitted. "But for what purpose?"

"To send him to paradise," Hassan answered. "Ali has been taken to a remote area, where he will awake to find himself in a lovely garden with music, wine and charming female companions."

"No wonder those poor devils follow you," Fawzi said, unable to conceal his grudging respect for the cult leader's cunning or his contempt for the man's actions. "You've even made a falsehood of death."

"Truth is relative," Hassan said, shrugging.

"Not entirely," the colonel replied. "You won't be able to resurrect the men you sent to take care of Katzenelenbogen and his imported team of commandos."

"That is unfortunate," Hassan said. "I don't know what went wrong at the airport or later at that construction site."

"Both ambushes failed because your men were pitted against professionals," Fawzi answered. "You should spend more time instructing your people how to fight instead of concentrating on this religious charade."

"But that's essential to the success of my organization," Hassan told him. "My Assassins are absolutely obedient, totally fearless...."

"And incompetent," Fawzi snapped. "Your Assassins are drug addicts. That imbecile Mehmet Ali Agca had probably been smoking opium before he tried to assassinate the Pope. No wonder the idiot failed. He even held his gun in an absurd overhead position to try to shoot over the crowd."

"None of my people will be taken alive," Hassan stated. "True, we underestimated these foreigners, but they're not important."

"Your spy among the Israelis seems to think otherwise," Fawzi commented. "He says that damned one-armed Jew is something of a legend, an expert at finding his enemies and destroying them.''

"I am aware of my men's apprehension concerning this Katzenelenbogen," Hassan said with a sigh, weary of the conversation. "But I fail to see how five men can make any difference. We knew we'd have to deal with Israel's own intelligence and military personnel. That didn't stop us. How great a concern can five men be?''

"Five extraordinary men," Fawzi remarked.

"My group leader in Israel will take care of them," Hassan assured him. "Our main target remains the prime minister.''

"I only wish I could be there to see that Jewish pig die," Fawzi said bitterly.

NASSER FAWZI was born in 1943 in a village near Deir Yassin in Palestine. His father was a peasant goat farmer who also sold yogurt to people in and around the community of Deir Yassin.

When Nasser was five years old, he was stricken with pneumonia. His mother and father took him to a nearby Red Cross station for treatment. He never saw his parents again.

While he was being treated, his village was wiped out by Jewish Irgun terrorists. Red Cross representatives actually witnessed the massacre; two hundred fifty Arabs were killed.

Nasser Fawzi was adopted by a family of Palestinians who fled to Syria. The boy's sorrow over the death of his parents turned to hatred and a desire to inflict suffering on the people of Israel.

In 1958, an army captain named Ahmed Jibril formed a nucleus of the PFLP. Fifteen-year-old Nasser Fawzi eagerly volunteered to join the group. The Syrian terrorists launched a series of commando-style raids into Israel, attacking numerous kibbutz settlements, murdering dozens of Jews.

Jibril's group acquired a reputation as the most vicious of the *fedayeen* organizations. He broke off all relations with the Marxist, George Habbash, because he considered Habbash to be a weakling. Jibril even criticized Yasser Arafat for being a moderate who would never be militant enough to destroy the Jews.

Jibril believed in action, not words. He proved just how ruthless he could be in 1970 when he launched a rocket into an Israeli school bus, murdering nine children. The world, including most Arab nations, condemned this cruel, inexcusable atrocity. Nasser Fawzi applauded it and continued to follow Jibril.

Then Fawzi discovered that Jibril's true allegiance was to the Soviet Union. Jibril—like George Habbash, Mohammed Salameh and many other terrorist leaders—had been trained at the Patrice Lummumba University in Russia. He had a KGB "control" who operated from the Soviet Embassy in Beirut. Jibril was serving Moscow's interests in the Middle East, not the interests of the Arab people.

Thus Fawzi broke with the PLF and formed his own terrorist organization—the United Arab

Front. Dedicated to uniting all Arab nations to crush Israel, it proved to be even more radical and vicious than Jibril's group.

Fawzi considered himself a realist. After Israel was destroyed, the Arabs would have to remain united under a Marxist government. The new united Arab states would still do business with the Soviets, although they would have to take care not to give the Russians a chance to seize control. The capitalist West would be shunned, especially the United States, which could not be forgiven for supporting Israel.

Fawzi, however, found little backing for his plan. Even the majority of Arab terrorists realized the scheme was absurd. Ironically, the Soviets were one of Fawzi's few allies. Moscow regarded the UAF as a tiny group of lunatics, too small to cause any conflicts large enough to worry Mother Russia. The Russians felt certain the UAF would be shot down, so supplying them with arms would only help contribute to the turmoil the Kremlin wanted in the Middle East.

Since Fawzi could not get the Arab nations to see the "wisdom" of his plan against the Jews, there seemed to be only one alternative: he decided to incite a war between Israel and Egypt in the hope that the rest of the Middle East would be unable to avoid getting involved.

"ARE YOU CERTAIN nothing will go wrong this time?" Fawzi asked Hassan.

"The man ordered to kill the prime minister

has been specially trained for this sort of mission," the Assassin chief assured him. "I should have used him in the beginning. He's an explosives expert."

"It won't be easy for him to plant a bomb. . . ."

"That will not be a problem," Hassan said.

"What do you mean?" Fawzi demanded. "The Jew will be well protected. Security will be very strict."

"Do not worry, Colonel," Hassan urged. "The prime minister is as good as dead. As a matter of fact, you'll even get your wish."

"My wish?" Fawzi said, frowning.

"To see the Israeli die," Hassan replied. "You can watch it tomorrow morning—on television."

12

"So what's a nice Jewish girl like you doing in a place like this?" Rafael Encizo asked with grin.

"I can't believe you actually said that," Rachel Stern replied with a laugh. "What a line."

The couple were seated at a table in the Shaldag Inn, a restaurant with a reputation for having the best seafood in Tel Aviv.

"Ah," the Cuban remarked, "I see you do know how to laugh. I was afraid you had lost the ability. You always seem so serious."

"I'm in a serious business," the girl replied, using her fork to cut off a piece of *karpyon*. Israelis consider carp a delicacy.

"How did you become involved in this line of work?" the Cuban inquired.

"I was born in Israel," Rachel began, "which means I was exposed to several languages since childhood. By the time I was eighteen, I spoke Hebrew, English and French fluently. In the military, they taught me Arabic as well. I served as a translator in 1973 when Egyptian soldiers crossed the Suez Canal to try and seize control of Sinai. That reinforced my belief that Israeli must always be ready to deal with aggression."

"It's been said that Sadat launched the invasion largely to prove that Egypt wasn't the military pushover she appeared after the Six Day War," Encizo commented.

"I suppose you believe that even then, Sadat was planning to propose peace with Israel?" Rachel clucked her tongue in disgust.

"I think it's possible," the Cuban answered. "If Sadat hadn't proven that Egypt could fight, he would have made the peace offer under weak conditions and lost face with the other Arab leaders. Don't forget, after he replaced Nasser as president, Sadat broke off Egypt's ties with the Soviet Union and kicked about seventeen-thousand Russian advisors out of his country. Anybody who tells Moscow to go to hell deserves some credit."

"You think that all evil comes from the Kremlin?" Rachel inquired.

"I know a lot of it does," Encizo replied. "I was captured by Castro's troops after the Bay of Pigs fiasco. They sent me to El Principe, a political prison where I was starved and tortured. When that didn't work, they forced me to stay awake for three days and nights to wear me down. Besides questioning me about the attempted invasion, they also tried to 're-educate' me. Russian 'technicians' supervised this behavior reconditioning to try and get me to embrace communism.

"I was told that the only hope for the oppressed masses was through Marxist-Leninism under the wise leadership of Comrade Fidel and

Nikita Khrushchev. I resisted for a while and then pretended to have a change of political heart," the Cuban continued. "I agreed with their bullshit and they rewarded me. I was allowed to sleep. The beatings stopped and I received more food."

"How'd you get out of there?" she asked.

"They got careless with me after they thought I was responding to their re-education. I eventually got a chance to jump a guard. I broke his neck and escaped. That's a rather long story. A damn good one, but long."

"You'll have to tell me some time," Rachel said. "Please don't misunderstand me. I also hate the Russians."

There was a lull in the conversation. Rafael finally broke it.

"I didn't invite you to dinner to discuss politics."

"Why did you ask me to have dinner with you?" Rachel inquired, raising an eyebrow.

"You're a fascinating lady," he replied. "A combination of beauty and intelligence."

"What interests you the most, Rafael?"

"Do I have to choose one?"

"How does *kafeh Turkee* sound for dessert?" Rachel asked. "It's Turkish coffee."

"Changing the subject?" the Cuban asked.

"For now."

THE COUPLE TOOK A TAXI to the November Apartments building. Encizo and Rachel entered the building. A brief elevator trip took them to the twelfth floor. They emerged in a corridor, deserted except for a janitor who was sweeping the floor.

"I'll see you to your door," Encizo told the woman.

"That's not necessary," she said.

"Of course it isn't, but I'm a bit old-fashioned about such things."

"You're quite a fellow, Rafael," she said as they strolled down the corridor.

Rachel led the way to her apartment. She inserted a key into the door, unlocked it, then turned to face Encizo.

"I really had a nice evening and I do like you, Rafael," she said. "But it isn't wise to get close to anyone when you're involved in this sort of work."

"Afraid of being hurt?" Encizo asked.

"Something like that," she admitted.

"That's part of life no matter what you do," the Cuban stated. "When you allow yourself to care about anyone, you take the risk of getting hurt."

He cupped Rachel's face in his hands and pressed his lips to hers in a brief, yet tender kiss. Rachel resisted for a moment, then responded in kind. Encizo gently broke contact.

"Good night, Rafael," she said. "And thank you."

The woman entered her room. Encizo waited until she closed the door before he turned to leave. The sound of a fist striking flesh, followed by Rachel's cry of pain, immediately drew him back to the door.

"Allah akbar," a voice shouted from behind the Cuban.

Encizo pivoted, drawing his Walther PPK from shoulder leather as he turned to face the new threat. The Arab janitor lunged at him, a dagger raised for attack.

Encizo fired into the charging assailant. A .380 dum-dum round punched into the Arab's chest, but it did not even slow him down. He closed in and thrust the knife at Encizo's chest. The Cuban barely sidestepped in time to avoid the poison-stained blade.

The Cuban seized the Assassin's forearm before the man could use the knife again. Encizo jammed the muzzle of his Walther under the Arab's chin and pulled the trigger. A 95-grain slug tore through the hollow of the killer's jaw, sliced his tongue and split the roof of his mouth.

Encizo shoved the twitching corpse aside. The terrorist dropped to the floor. The Cuban turned back to Rachel's apartment. The door burst open and another wild-eyed Assassin leaped at Encizo.

Both men crashed into a wall. The PPK was jarred from Encizo's grasp. The steel blade of a dagger flashed in the terrorist's fist as he swung the weapon at the Cuban's throat. Encizo jerked away from the knife.

Encizo's hand snaked out and caught the Assassin's wrist. He twisted the knife away from his throat and tried to drive a knee into the man's groin. He struck a thigh muscle. The terrorist struggled violently. Encizo rammed a fist under the man's ribs.

The killer grabbed Encizo's throat, his thumb digging into windpipe. The Cuban gave his opponent two more rib shots. The Assassin groaned and his grip loosened. The Phoenix Force defender clubbed the Arab's forearm with his fist to break the killer's choke-hold.

Encizo swung his elbow into the man's face. The terrorist's cheekbone cracked from the force of the blow, yet his head hardly moved from the impact. He savagely pumped a knee into Encizo's abdomen. The Cuban gasped but still held on to the wrist behind the killer's knife as both men stumbled away from the wall.

The Cuban heard voices of utter surprise and alarm as nearby tenants peered from their doorways. He suddenly bent his knees and abruptly lowered himself backward. His left thigh and buttock hit the floor as he pulled the startled terrorist forward.

The Cuban's right foot caught the man in the midriff. He rolled back, pumping his leg to send the killer sailing overhead in a judo circle-throw. The Assassin crashed to the floor. Encizo immediately leaped to his feet and reached for the Gerber Mark I he had strapped to his ankle.

With a snarl, the terrorist rose from the floor and angrily lunged at Encizo, thrusting the dagger at the Cuban's chest. Encizo waited for the charge then slashed the Gerber at his attacker.

The razor-sharp, double-edged fighting knife sliced through flesh and muscle. The Assassin screamed and dropped his dagger as blood spurted from severed arteries in his wrist.

The Cuban's tactic caught the terrorist completely off guard. Stunned and disoriented, the Arab made a wild grab for Encizo's knife. The Phoenix Force pro feinted a quick jab with the Gerber to distract his opponent. Then Encizo executed a lightning-fast backhand slash that caught the terrorist under the jawline.

Sharp steel split open the man's throat. Blood gushed from the horrible wound. The Arab fell to his knees, hands groping at his neck in a hopeless attempt to stop his life from spilling out. He failed. The Assassin fell on his face and died.

Tenants were screaming for the police. A sergeant in the Israeli reserves emerged from his room with a .45 Colt 1911A1 in his fist. Encizo heard the man shout something in Hebrew.

Encizo did not even bother to turn around to see what the Israeli wanted. He bolted for Rachel's apartment, fearful that the woman might already have come to harm.

The Phoenix Force warrior found Rachel struggling with another Arab assailant. The Assassin had pinned Rachel to the floor and was trying to strangle her. The woman fought well. She raked her nails across the man's face. The killer screamed in agony as blood oozed from a torn eyeball. The bastard may have been wired in drugs, but nothing could make him immune to such fiery pain.

Furious, the terrorist raised a fist to strike the woman. Encizo grabbed the man's arm before he could throw a punch. The Cuban yanked the terrorist off Rachel and slammed a knee under the Arab's jaw.

The man's head bounced backward from the blow. Encizo immediately thrust the point of his Gerber into the hollow of the Assassin's exposed throat. The man's mouth fell open and blood spewed out. The terrorist sprawled on the carpet, his body trembling. Then all trace of life ceased and the man lay still with Encizo's knife still buried in his throat.

"Rachel," Encizo said as he knelt beside her. "Are you okay?"

"It's nothing I won't get over," she replied, rubbing her bruised jaw. "Your timing is excellent. How can I repay you?"

Suddenly the Israeli sergeant appeared in the doorway and aimed his .45 at Encizo. The man snapped a command in Hebrew. Encizo did not know what it meant, but he decided it would not hurt to raise his hands.

"You might start by telling this fella what happened," Encizo told Rachel.

13

"Katzenelenbogen," the prime minister greeted when he saw the Phoenix Force leader entering his hospital room. "I was told you were here."

"How are you feeling, sir?" Yakov inquired as he closed the door.

"Like I recently had a heart attack," the prime minister said, smiling weakly.

He lay in a large bed. The back section was raised, allowing him to sit up. Katz noted the Israeli's sickly pale color. He seemed very, very tired.

"The last time we spoke was two years ago, correct?" the prime minister remarked.

"Yes," Katz replied. "I'm sure you know what I want to speak with you about, sir."

"I've been told that someone tried to kill me. That is not a new experience for me. People have been trying to kill me for half a century. I'm not going to start worrying about that now."

"You're aware that the assassins were Egyptians?" Katz asked.

"That is what I've been told."

"A lot of people in your administration think

the government in Cairo sent the killers. Do you believe that?''

''No, I do not believe President Mubarak would send assassins to kill me.''

''I don't believe it either,'' Katz told him. ''I have reason to suspect we're up against a highly efficient clandestine organization with agents scattered throughout the Middle East.''

''The Russians?'' the prime minister said, frowning as he adjusted his eyeglasses.

''No,'' Katz said. ''I think we're dealing with a different kind of clandestine network... older by centuries than the KGB. An independent intelligence branch with no political allegiance, consisting of fanatics who are totally loyal to a false religious leader who is in fact a cunning mercenary.''

''How melodramatic,'' the prime minister said. ''They certainly sound colorful.''

''I don't know if I'd call the Order of the Assassins colorful,'' Katz said. ''Are you familiar with the history of the Hashishins?''

''I know they haven't been active for more than two hundred years.''

''I have reason to believe someone has managed to revive it.''

''What proof do you have?''

Katz explained the incidents that had occurred since Phoenix Force arrived in Israel. ''I just identified the star-shaped tattoo found on several of the dead terrorists,'' he continued. ''It is the mark of an initiate in the Order of the Assassins.''

"A crude star can mean anything, Yakov," the prime minister replied.

"The emblem on the *bruss* shirts—and the amulet is also an Assassin symbol," the colonel stated. "The sign of the Order."

"That proves that the Arab terrorists involved may have adopted some Assassin symbols," the prime minister said. "The swastika was originally a symbol of enlightment in Asia, yet the Nazis chose it for their party emblem."

"Damn it," Katz snapped. "You're the most stubborn man I've ever met. Why are you fighting me about this?"

"Because we have to consider all possibilities, Colonel," the prime minister answered. "What other proof do you have?"

"The members of the Assassins have traditionally come from the Ismailis Muslim sect," Katz said. "We've checked with the personnel computers and discovered that most of the terrorists who we've killed in battle have been Ismailis. Several were also listed as security risks due to fanatical behavior in the past. Major Nizam, the Egyptian security officer sent to help us, contacted Cairo and checked on the Egyptian terrorists involved. All were Ismailis Muslims."

"That's all circumstantial evidence," the prime minister remarked. "However, it is more convincing when it is linked together. But, as I recall, the Assassins were a mercenary outfit. Who would have hired them?"

"Probably a terrorist outfit," Katz answered.

"We don't have enough details yet to make an educated guess."

"You may be right," the prime minister admitted.

"Your Mossad director doesn't believe it's possible," Yakov said. "And he thinks I'm paranoid because I'm convinced there's a spy in one of the intelligence networks—either Mossad or Sheruth Modiin."

"He thinks the Egyptians are behind it?"

"Yes," Katz confirmed. "If you're assassinated, there's a good chance Mossad will retaliate against Egypt. If enough members of Parliament agree to a major military action, Israel could go to war...."

"Your honesty is always refreshing, Yakov," the prime minister laughed. "You're not really concerned about me. The possibility that my assassination could lead to war is what worries you."

"I am concerned about your safety, sir," Katz corrected. "But one life—yours, mine, anyone's—is not as important as preserving our peace with Egypt. We can't allow Israel to be tricked into an unjust war."

"I agree, Colonel," the prime minister answered. "And I will tell everyone what I think at the press conference tomorrow morning—the conference your Canadian friend tried to talk me out of."

"I don't think you should have a conference at this time either, sir," Katz stated. "You're well protected here at the clinic. You're safer here."

"Safe?" the prime minister said. "No one is ever safe. We thought we were safe huddled together in the ghettos of Europe. Protection in numbers. Safe in our own segregated communities. The Nazis showed us how wrong we were. No one is *ever* safe."

"There's no point in inviting death," Katz said. "You shouldn't have that press conference unless you have a burning desire to become a martyr."

"Would you call Anwar Sadat a martyr?"

"No one had warned Sadat not to attend that military parade in Nasr City. He had no reason to suspect anyone would try to gun him down that day. I'm warning you now, sir. Just give us a few days and I'm sure we'll be able to locate the Assassins and destroy them."

"I appreciate your concern," the prime minister said. "But I must insist on the press conference."

"God in Heaven." Katz rolled his eyes toward the ceiling. "You're stubbornness is infuriating. You mentioned Sadat. He risked his life in an effort to make peace with Israel. He was probably murdered for that very reason. Is your reply to his courage and sacrifice to jeopardize the peace treaty by this bullheaded insistence to have a press conference?"

"It is because of the memory of Anwar Sadat that I must have the conference," the prime minister answered. "I will publicly state that there was an assassination attempt and that it was not the work of the Egyptian government. I won't mention your theory about the Assassins, but I will state that a terrorist organization is responsible. Everyone must know that Egypt and Israel shall remain allies.''

''The speech can wait a day or two longer.''

''No it can't,'' the prime minister insisted. ''I might be dead in a day or two. There is no way to be certain the assassins can't kill me in this very bed or that my heart will hold out two more days.''

Katz sighed, knowing it was futile to try and change the prime minister's mind.

14

Gary Manning adjusted the straps of the borrowed shoulder-holster rig and checked the Eagle .357 Magnum pistol. Unlike McCarter, Manning favored a rifle to a handgun. The Canadian had been good with a long gun ever since he started hunting rabbits with a .22 rifle as a youth.

When Manning had to use a handgun, he liked Magnums because of their long range and reliable knock-down power. He had carried various types of Magnum revolvers such as the Colt Python and the S&W .41 Mag. The Canadian had never handled the Eagle until he test-fired it at the Mossad indoor range.

The Eagle handled well. It resembled a Colt .45 Government Model but was different because the gun featured a 9-round magazine and fired .357 cartridges. A product of the Israeli Military Industries INC—the Eagle featured combat sights, an adjustable trigger-pull and an ambidextrous safety.

Manning slid the pistol into the leather sheath under his arm and flipped the transmit switch for a radio-communications set on the desk. He picked up the microphone.

"Centaur One," he said, speaking into the mike. "This is Control. Do you read me. Over."

"Glad to see you haven't fallen asleep, Control," David McCarter replied through the loudspeaker. "Read you loud and clear. Over."

The Briton was piloting a Westland Lynx helicopter, patroling the sky around the area of the Straus Medical Center. McCarter was scanning the ground and buildings below, searching for any suspicious individuals who might be armed with rocket launchers, mortars or other weapons with a long-range capacity capable of presenting a threat to the prime minister.

"Anything yet? Over," Manning asked.

"Negative," the Briton replied. "Everything is as quiet as a cemetery. Over."

"Okay. Catch you later. Over." The Canadian changed frequencies before he transmitted again. "Centaur Two, do you read? Over."

"Centaur Two," a voice replied. "Nothing has changed here, sir. Over."

The second guard post consisted of several Israeli troops on foot patrol around the hospital with special emphasis on the rose garden, where the prime minister would deliver his speech.

"Okay," Manning told Centaur Two. "You guys have had a long night. You'll be relieved in a few more minutes. Stay alert. Over and out."

Manning made one more call. "Cyclops, this is Control. Do you read? Over?"

"Cyclops here," Keio Ohara answered. "You're quite clear. Any news, Control? Over."

"Negative," the Canadian said. "Centaur One and Two haven't detected anything. How about you?"

Ohara was in charge of supervising the surveillance equipment in the garden. Several cameras had been set up in the area as well as heat detectors and a Land Sonar Wave device designed to register movement.

"Nothing at all," the Japanese stated. "Over."

"Maybe Katz is wrong about this," Manning muttered, speaking into the microphone before he realized he still had it in his hand.

"Perhaps," Ohara said without conviction, well aware that Yakov's hunches were seldom wrong.

The Canadian moved the microphone and hissed a single four-letter word in disgust. He had been careless. One does not transmit doubts to the troops in the field. Manning reached for the coffee pot and poured himself a fresh cup.

"The main event will be in two hours, Cyclops," he announced. "Better have somebody else take over the spy gear and get ready to meet the press. Over."

"Right," Ohara replied. "See you then. Over and out."

MANNING WATCHED THE REPORTERS enter the rose garden. Keio Ohara was concentrating on the television personnel, inspecting their camera equipment for hidden firearms or explosives. Manning handled the print journalists.

He took extra care with the Egyptian journalist in the group, carefully checking his ID and comparing the photo with the face.

"I see security is quite strict since the assassination attempt," Abdul Munsul remarked in thickly accented English as Manning expertly frisked the Egyptian.

"I hope you understand," the Canadian said, looking at the man's cassette tape recorder. "Mind if I have a look at that?"

"Of course not," Monsul said, handing Manning the recorder.

Manning unscrewed the bolts from the back plate of the recorder and checked inside. He found only circuits, transistors and four size-C batteries. The Canadian put the plate back in place and tightened the screws before he returned it to Monsul.

"Everything okay?" the Egyptian asked.

"Sorry for the trouble," Manning replied.

The Israeli prime minister soon emerged from the hospital. Surrounded by Mossad bodyguards, he shuffled to the center of the garden, where the news representatives had formed a semicircle around a podium. The prime minister stepped behind the lecture stand and prepared to address the assembly.

Manning continued to suspiciously scan the area. The veteran warrior's sixth sense was setting off a silent alarm. The fear that he had overlooked something important nagged at him as he watched Keio Ohara at the opposite side of the garden. The Japanese turned to face Manning and nodded to assure him everything was all right.

"Hope you're right, pal," Manning commented as he unhooked a walkie-talkie from his belt.

Ohara saw him and followed his lead. Manning pressed the switch. "Keio?"

"Right here," Ohara answered. "Anything wrong?"

"Nothing I can put my finger on," Manning admitted. "Are you sure all those TV cameras are safe?"

"Absolutely," Ohara confirmed. "I even checked the podium and microphones for booby traps. All clean."

"I'd feel better if you headed back to the surveillance center to man the controls there," Manning said. "You're the best man for that sort of thing."

"Very well," the Japanese replied. "You can handle everything here?"

"I'm not exactly alone," Manning said. "Mossad has agents posted all over the garden, and Rafael is out in the parking lot checking vehicles as they come in."

"Might check with him," Ohara suggested. "I haven't heard from him since we got out here."

"Neither have I." Manning frowned. "I'll get in touch with him. Contact me if anything shows up on the spy cameras."

"You know it," the Japanese promised as he left.

Manning pressed the button of his transceiver and tried to contact Encizo.

There was no reply.

Manning tried again.

"Rafael? Do you read me?"

"I'm here, Gary," the Cuban answered.

"Had me worried for a minute," Manning admitted.

"My walkie-talkie didn't want to talkie," Encizo said. "I had to borrow one from a Mossad agent to answer you."

"Everything looks okay so far," Manning said. "Any problems out there?"

"Not yet," Encizo said. "We just stopped a couple of Arab reporters and checked them out. They're Egyptians, so we made double sure they weren't armed before we let them go."

"Egyptians?" Manning questioned. "But there's already an Egyptian here. I checked him out myself. Free-lance guy named Monsul."

"Should I detain these two just in case?" the Cuban asked.

Gary Manning scanned the faces of the journalists in the garden, looking for Abdul Monsul. He did not see the Egyptian among the men seated before the prime minister. The Israeli leader began his speech, first in Hebrew and then in English.

"You have all heard of the attempt on my life," the prime minister declared. "You may have heard that two Egyptians were involved. In fact, these would-be assassins were terrorists with no connection to the friendly government in Cairo. Be warned enemies of peace, you will not turn Israel and Egypt against each other. . . .''

Then Manning located Monsul. The Egyptian sat on a bench apart from the other journalists. He had the cassette recorder in his lap with the back plate removed. The Canadian frowned. He had checked that recorder and found nothing suspicious. Could he have missed something?

"Gary?" Encizo called via the walkie-talkie in the Canadian's hand.

"I'm here," Manning spoke hastily.

"For a second I thought this radio also had run-down batteries," the Cuban remarked.

"Batteries," Manning whispered. "The goddamn batteries."

Abdul Monsul removed the four size-C batteries from the back of his tape recorder. He smiled. Soon he would be in paradise for eternity after he completed his holy mission for Lord Hassan. It was the will of Allah that the infidel leader should die and Abdul Monsul had been chosen to dispatch the Jew devil to hell.

He unscrewed the top off the first battery. It contained less than three ounces of C-4 plastic explosives. Monsul removed the top off another battery that had a similar charge of C-4. The third battery contained a tiny plunger-style detonator, two copper wires and a slender size-AA battery. Finally, he unscrewed the last battery and gingerly extracted two special blasting caps. Monsul attached the wires to the caps and inserted them into the C-4. Then he hooked the wires to the detonator and fitted the tiny AA battery into the base of the electrical squib.

The explosives were ready.

Monsul deposited the device in his coat pocket and rose from the bench. All he had to do was get close enough to the prime minister to be certain the blast would be fatal. To detonate the bomb, Monsul simply had to push the plunger to the squib—then he himself, the Jew and anyone else who happened to be too close would be blown to bits. Allah would receive Abdul's soul and reward him for his devotion to the true faith. Lord Hassan had told him of this, and there could be no doubt that his word was the one great truth.

Monsul walked toward the prime minister's podium. He was so pleased with his divine mission and confident that God guided his every footstep, he failed to notice Gary Manning as the Canadian crept up behind him.

Monsul was closing in on a suitable striking distance.

Manning swiftly drew the Eagle pistol and slammed the steel barrel across the terrorist's mastoid bone, behind his left ear. The Assassin crumbled to the ground. The Phoenix Force commando dragged Monsul into the nearest cluster of bushes. He frisked the unconscious terrorist and found the miniature bomb in Monsul's pocket.

The Canadian removed a set of riot cuffs from

his jacket and quickly bound the Arab's wrists behind his back. Then he unclipped the walkie-talkie from his belt and pressed the button.

"Keio, Rafael. A party crasher showed up."

"Are you sure?" Encizo asked.

"Positive," Manning said. "No problem. Tell Katz we've got a live one. Now we just have to keep him that way."

15

"Where the hell is Katzenelenbogen?" Deputy Director Geller demanded as he entered the office of Colonel Joshua Ben-David, head of the medical section of Mossad. "I was told I could find him here."

"Yes, sir," Ben-David said as he rose from his desk. "He and two of his men brought a patient in here about half an hour ago."

"A patient?" Geller frowned. "Another one of his foreign friends?"

"The director told me that information about the man, including his name, is on a need-to-know level," Ben-David replied. "I'm afraid you are not authorized to receive such information."

"By God, where is that arrogant son of a bitch?" Geller snapped.

"The director?" Ben-David asked with raised eyebrows.

"Katzenelenbogen, damn it."

"Right here, Mr. Geller," Yakov announced as he entered the office. "What seems to be the problem?"

"*You're* my problem," Geller fired, glaring at

the one-armed colonel. "You went over my head to the director, didn't you?"

"I contacted the director because I have reason to believe there's a double agent among either Mossad or Sheruth Modiin."

"Are you saying you suspect me of being an enemy agent?" Geller demanded.

"Yes," Yakov said.

"How dare you," Geller said. "Who gave you the right to pass judgement on me?"

"I didn't say you're guilty," Katz explained. "But you are a suspect. My interests are for the safety of the prime minister, the preservation of Israel and avoiding a conflict that could lead to the Third World War. I'm afraid your ego doesn't rate very high compared to that."

"*My* ego," Geller spat. "You have the conceit to decide that only you can handle this situation. You're still a member of Mossad, yet you import those goyim. You call yourself a Jew, but you trust those four more than your own people."

"You're talking like a fool," Katz said.

"Right now you've got the director and even the prime minister convinced that you're going to solve this business and save the world," Geller continued angrily. "But when this is over, I'm going to see to it that disciplinary action is taken against you."

"I'll worry about that when this is over," Katz said. "For now, I'd like to talk to doctor Ben-David in private."

"Fine," Geller said tensely. "I'll have a chat

with the director and perhaps with the deputy prime minister as well.''

Geller turned and stomped out of the office. Colonel Ben-David sighed as he turned to Katz.

''I trust you realize he can make a lot of trouble for you, Colonel.''

''He'll try,'' Katz agreed.

''He may succeed,'' Ben-David warned. ''Don't underestimate him. And don't forget that politics can be as sinister as espionage. One is apt to forget that Israel has a president as well as a prime minister. There has been some hard feeling between the two leaders. The prime minister and his deputy aren't the best of friends either.''

''You're suggesting that Parliament might decide the prime minister is not capable of serving in his present office because of his physical and mental condition after so many heart attacks?'' Katz shook his head. ''I doubt that.''

''Or they could cast doubt on your loyalty to Israel,'' Ben-David said bluntly. ''I trust you. I've heard a lot about you, Colonel Katz. You're an old war-horse who has fought a thousand battles. You know the horror of war and you don't want to see it happen again.''

''There will always be wars and fighting,'' Katz stated. ''I think we all know that one day there will be a major war in the Middle East, but we have to do whatever possible to postpone that day.''

''And the fellow you brought here, this Abdul Monsul, can help us in this matter?''

"It's possible," Katz answered. "That's why we need to interrogate him with scopolamine to make certain he tells us the truth."

"I've checked the blood samples we took from Monsul," Ben-David sighed. "Are you aware he's a drug addict?"

"Yes," Katz answered. "We found tablets of synthetic heroin in his pocket, and I'm certain he smoked a good deal of hashish. Probably took other drugs as well."

"That's an understatement," Ben-David declared. "We found traces of cocaine, various depressants and strong stimulants as well. On top of that, you've ordered that we keep Monsul under sedation because you claim he'll commit suicide if he's conscious."

"That's true. He was also carrying a cyanide capsule."

"We could keep him in restraints," the doctor suggested.

"When we captured one of his comrades, we used riot cuffs, and that didn't stop him from killing himself. If Monsul isn't sedated, he'll do his damnest to take his own life. I wouldn't be surprised if he bit off his own tongue."

"That man's constitution has gone through hell," Ben-David said. "He's been abusing all types of drugs for years. I don't think his heart will be able to take a large injection of scopolamine."

"What would you say the odds are, Doctor?"

"About eighty percent that the scopolamine would kill him," Ben-David answered grimly.

"Is there any other drug we could use?"

"Sodium pentothal. It's much safer, but not as reliable."

"Perhaps we should try something else," Katz mused thoughtfully.

ABDUL MONSUL heard the mellow song made by water gently running along a stream. Birds chirped and a cool breeze stroked his cheek. A lyre was being played in the distance.

Monsul opened his eyes. A ceiling of eucalyptus branches hung overheard. The Arab glanced about. A fresh spring ran between the trees. He turned his head and saw a lovely young woman. Dressed in a transparent silk garment with a veil draped across her face, she knelt and offered him a platter of figs, dates and sliced fruit.

"Paradise," Monsul said as he sat up. "Allah has rewarded me."

"Indeed, true believer," a voice announced in Arabic. "You have arrived."

Monsul gazed up at two men clad in white robes and *keffiyeh*. Both had white beards, yet their faces were unlined and their eyes glowed with the health of youth. Monsul rose from the carpet of grass. He suddenly noticed he too was wearing a fine robe of white silk.

"Is it not written in the Koran: 'Enter unto paradise; no fear be with you, nor have you sorrow'?" one of the bearded men declared. "Welcome, true believer."

"Praise Allah," Monsul replied. "But who are

you who greet me in this wondrous place of peace and beauty?"

"We were once men not unlike yourself," a robed man replied. "But we were then prophets of Allah. I am Ishmael and this is the Imam Muwafig."

"Ishmael," Monsul cried. "I followed your teachings, great prophet...."

"You followed me not," the bearded man who called himself Ishmael said sadly. "Nor did you follow Allah. Instead, you followed the word of a cunning liar and fraud."

"But Hassan is your voice on earth," the startled Monsul began.

"That is his claim," Muwafig replied. "But it is not true. Hassan duped you, poor soul."

"But he first showed me paradise," Monsul said.

"He showed you sorcery," Ishmael explained. "Hassan is a devil who misled you by using Satan's evil magic."

"I am confused," Monsul said.

"The very first verse of the Koran speaks of Allah, the merciful and the compassionate," Ishmael stated. "Did you ever consider this when Hassan instructed you to hate and kill for him? Could his word truly be the word of God?"

Monsul began to weep.

"Do not despair," Ishmael urged. "Allah will not damn you for following a false prophet. Your mind was corrupt, yet your heart remained pure."

"I have wronged the one true God," Monsul moaned. "Yet Allah forgives me?"

"Yes, believer," Muwafig said. "But you must redeem yourself."

"Anything," Monsul cried. "I will do anything."

"What do you last remember of your life on earth?" Muwafig asked.

"I was sent to kill the Jewish prime minister," Monsul said. "I was about to carry out my mission, but I don't recall what happened then."

"You were struck down by a lightning bolt," Ishmael explained. "Your heart stopped beating. You died before you could harm the Israeli."

"Allah be praised," Monsul sighed with relief. "Then the Jew was not meant to die?"

"Allah also created the Jews," Ishmael said. "He must have a reason."

"But Jews are unbelievers...."

"Do you claim to understand the mind of God?" Ishmael demanded. "Only He is the Lord of the day of doom. Judgment is His to make. It was never meant for you."

"What shall I do?"

"The Israelis have taken your body to a room of the dead," Muwafig explained. "Your life will be restored and you will speak with them. Tell the Jews everything you know about Hassan and his followers."

"Tell the Jews?" Monsul sighed. "Very well."

"May Allah bless you," Ishmael said with a smile.

Monsul suddenly felt a sting in the back of his neck. He winced and reached for the pain's source. Ishmael caught his wrist.

"Do not worry," he whispered. "You are about to return. There will be little pain. Relax. . . ."

Monsul nodded in reply. He felt light-headed and giddy. Then his knees buckled and he fell to the ground. Seconds later, he lay at the feet of the robed figures. As Monsul slept peacefully, a hand plucked the tranquilizer dart from his neck.

Gary Manning approached Monsul, an Anschutz .22-caliber air rifle in his fists. Colonel Katzenelenbogen followed him. "Ishmael" and "Muwafig" pulled off their false beards to reveal the faces of Major Nizam and Captain Malik, the two Egyptian security officers.

"You both played your roles magnificently," Katz told the pair.

"I don't understand why you needed us instead of playing this game yourself," Malik remarked. "You speak Arabic, Colonel Katz."

"My Arabic doesn't have a natural accent," Yakov explained. "You and the major speak the language as your native tongue. I could best serve this charade by listening and telling Gary when to fire the sleep dart."

"It also gave you an opportunity to observe us," Nizam said, smiling. "I trust it proved we can be trusted."

"Yes, Major," Katz assured him.

"What are your plans now?" Malik asked.

"We're going to take Abdul Monsul back to Mossad headquarters," Katz explained. "He'll awake in a morgue where everyone will reinforce the story of his heart attack in the rose garden. If our performance has convinced Monsul, he will tell us everything he knows about the Order of the Assassins."

"If we're ready to leave 'paradise,'" Rachel Stern remarked as she stripped off her veil. "May I change into something less embarrassing?"

"I don't know why you're embarrassed," Manning grinned. "You look great."

"Thanks," she said dryly.

"Well," Manning said, "so much for our stay in heaven. Now if we can find the location of the Assassins' headquarters, we can put these bastards out to pasture for good."

"We also have a double agent here in Israel to take care of," Katz added. "And we'd better find out who he is."

16

Demons with horns, serpentine tails and batlike wings leered and danced in the flickering flames. Bestial growls and groans emanated from the monstrous creatures.

Hassan opened the door and prepared to enter the room where the hideous beings lurked. He hesitated. The awful creatures seemed so very real. . . .

Hassan extended a shaky hand and placed it on the winged back of a scaly green monster. His fingers passed through the demon. Hassan smiled, amused by his own apprehension. He marched to the center of the room.

The demons surrounded him. Fangs hung from their mouths. Toadlike faces with yellow eyes, mocked him. Clawed hands with black talons slashed the air in threatening gestures. It all seemed so very real.

"Turn it off, Jemal," he ordered in a loud voice.

Suddenly the demons vanished. The fiery lights disappeared. The room was sent into peaceful darkness. Hassan groped for the door, but it opened and light from the corridor sliced into the cell. Jemal appeared in the doorway.

"It worked," Hassan told his manservant.
"Did you see it on the monitor?"

The servant nodded.

"Imagine how these ignorant dolts will react," Hassan said as he stepped into the hallway. "Surrounded by demons from hell. Those morons will beg me to rescue them."

He was very pleased with the new addition to his collection of tricks. The "demons"—images that appeared to be solid—were actually three-dimensional figures projected from a lens in the ceiling of the room. A sound track of roaring animals was played through a loudspeaker to complete the illusion.

The system had cost Hassan a small fortune but would be worth it. Now he could send his followers to hell as well as paradise. He could show them the rewards for blind faith in his word and the punishments for failing to obey him.

Manipulating people had always been Hassan's specialty. He had first learned the art of trickery as the son of a traveling magician in Iraq. The father-and-son team rode in their tiny wagon from province to province, setting up a tent in marketplaces.

Hassan's father was an expert at sleight of hand. He amazed people by producing coins from thin air, making melons disappear or pulling cloth from his clenched fist. Perhaps he was too good at his trade; eventually it cost him his life.

A trio of superstitious Shiite Muslims were

horrified when they saw Hassan's father perform the illusion of the burning stone. The magician held a rock in his palm and passed his other hand over it. The stone then appeared to burst into flame. The Shiite fanatics attacked the conjurer and stabbed him to death, convinced such magic was born of the devil.

His mother had died at childbirth. Young Hassan, now orphaned was alone in the world. He wandered the streets and was forced to beg to survive. A clever youth, he soon learned to use the skills of a magician to distract unsuspecting individuals as he deftly plucked their purses and wallets. He also discovered he could impress less worldly lads with simple tricks. By the time he was eleven, Hassan was the leader of a gang of young thieves and beggars, who coordinated with masterful skill to steal larger and more expensive merchandise.

Hassan despised any type of religion, blaming such beliefs for the death of his father. Yet he realized the tremendous influence of Islam in the Arab world. He decided that manipulating people through their religious notions was the best way to gain control over them.

The boy studied the Koran and the Bible. He quietly slipped into Mosques and churches of various religious sects and observed the services, trying to select the faith that seemed best suited for his scheme.

Hassan was nineteen years old when he read about the Order of the Assassins. It seemed he had found his destiny. The Hashishins had even been founded by a man with his name. What the original Hassan had done centuries ago, he could do again. And thus Hassan began his sinister, ruthless climb to power.

Twenty-six years later, Hassan became the leader of his own clandestine organization of fanatical killers. The new leader of the Assassins had even more ambition than his forerunner. Hassan planned to create a secret empire of followers, a world power that would exist in the shadows, yet would be capable of infiltrating governments, toppling nations and changing the course of history.

"HASSAN," Colonel Fawzi shouted as he stomped into the corridor. "I've been looking everywhere for you."

"You seem upset, Colonel," the cult leader replied.

"Of course I am," Fawzi snapped. "I watched the Israeli prime minister's press conference this morning."

"He isn't dead?" Hassan questioned.

"You didn't know that?" Fawzi was startled. "You mean you didn't even turn on a radio to listen for a news bulletin about the conference?"

"I've been busy with other matters," the Assassin leader said, shrugging.

"The Jew gave a flowery speech about what good friends Israel and Egypt are," Fawzi told Hassan. "He accused the 'terrorists' who tried to kill him of attempting to provoke a conflict between the two countries. It was a very moving speech. You should have heard it. The rest of the world did."

"That complicates matters," Hassan admitted.

"You talk as if this is a minor problem," Fawzi said as he began to pace the floor. "Your assassin obviously failed. He didn't even try to kill the Jew."

"Something must have happened to him," Hassan said. "The Mossad agents probably found his explosives. I was certain it would work...."

"You've always been certain your plans would work, you pompous ass," the terrorist colonel snapped. "You send your assassins out to kill for you, but they never succeed. Little wonder. They're nothing but a collection of morons whose brains have been rotted away by drugs and religious hogwash."

"They're totally dedicated to me..." Hassan said.

"Oh, yes," Fawzi snickered. "They're willing to die for you. Dying seems to be all they know how to do. They're good at getting themselves killed, but not worth a damn when it comes to killing anyone else. The United Arab Front hired you to assassinate the prime minister. Your people have failed."

"According to my agent in Israeli intelligence," Hassan said, "Colonel Katzenelenbogen and those damn foreigners are the problem."

"A problem your men have not been able to deal with," Fawzi complained.

"You didn't hire me to kill anyone except the Israeli prime minister."

"But you promised that your men would take care of anyone who got between them and the Jew."

"I made a mistake," Hassan confessed. "I underestimated Katzenelenbogen and his team. You were right, Colonel. They are special. We can deal with Israeli intelligence because we've penetrated them. We understand them and we can outguess them. But Katzenelenbogen realizes there's a spy in the Israeli intelligence structure, so his men have been working on their own. My agent can't get enough details about them to help us."

"Your people are no match for them," Fawzi declared. "My UAF soldiers will take care of Katzenelenbogen and his friends."

"I think that would be a mistake," Hassan warned. "If your men fail, it will just make matters worse. Even if they succeed, it won't make that much difference. The prime minister will still be alive."

"Perhaps with the Jew cripple and his team out of the way," Fawzi said, "your people will be able to accomplish their mission."

"Oh, they'll succeed," Hassan said. "My spy inside Israeli intelligence is going to see to that personally."

17

Rafael Encizo lay naked in the depths of Rachel Stern's warm, comfortable bed. He was thinking about the pleasures of the past while—such thoughts aroused him. The sound of bare feet padding into the room triggered him into action. Encizo's hand automatically reached toward the holstered Walther PPK that hung on the bedpost near his head. Then he saw the smooth curves and high breasts of the nude intruder.

"Don't shoot," Rachel teased. "I brought you a drink."

"Thanks," he said, running an inviting hand up her thigh as she climbed onto the bed beside him. He placed his drink on the night table as she propped a pillow behind her back and shook a cigarette from a pack. Rafael continued his admiring exploring.

"You've got a great touch," she said as she fired the smoke and inhaled deeply. "Crazy hormones and a great touch," she laughed.

Rachel and Rafael had made love several times. For both it had been a relaxing, wonderful respite from the high-pressure hell they had been submerged in. But Rafael, a man who had worked hard to earn a reputation as a woman's man, was not satisfied. Not *quite* satisfied.

He kissed her neck, softly, gently. He caressed her silky skin. Tenderly he held her. She snuffed out her smoke. Rafael smiled as Rachel Stern slipped her leg over his frame and kissed him hard on the mouth. It's starting again, he thought... *make it last*.

When they were finished, they held each other close, not wanting the real world to intrude. But eventually it had to happen. Rachel broke the silence.

"I suppose we'd better get ready to leave."

"I suppose," Rafael reluctantly agreed.

Soon the warrior's mind was back on business.

"Gary and Keio just got the sedan out of the shop today. New bullet-proof glass and complete bodywork with armor plating and a fresh coat of paint. They're driving it over here to pick us up."

"I still don't think it's necessary to move out of my apartment," Rachel stated. "The terrorists probably won't try anything here again."

"Let's not take any chances," Encizo told her, glancing at his Seiko Diver's wristwatch. "They'll be arriving any minute now."

"I hope we get a chance to do this again, Rafael," she said. "It was great."

The Cuban was in full agreement.

Rafael strapped on his shoulder-holster rig and made certain the Walther was ready for action. Then he wrapped a Velcro bandage around his ankle and strapped the Gerber Mark I sheath knife to it. Rachel had donned a khaki shirt and slacks. She opened the cylinders of her snub nose and checked the thirty-eight cartridges before returning the gun to her purse.

"I guess we're both ready for action," Encizo said. "Let's go."

Encizo and Rachel waited in the lobby until the sedan pulled in front of the November Apartments. They recognized Gary Manning's face behind the steering wheel and Keio Ohara seated beside him. The couple left the building and headed for the car.

Full auto fire exploded from the rooftop of a men's clothing store across the street from the November Apartments. Another salvo of copper-jacketed slugs snarled at them from a newsstand on the street corner. A third stream of deadly 7.62mm rounds sizzled from a cab that had pulled up to the curb behind the sedan.

Caught in a three-way cross fire, the sedan was pelted by dozens of bullets. Manning and Ohara felt as if they were trapped inside a tin can in the middle of a hailstorm. The armored body of the car rang sourly as bullets struck metal. The reinforced glass began to crack, threatening to give way under the bombardment of slugs.

Encizo and Rachel found themselves in an even deadlier situation. The couple were on the sidewalk, totally exposed to the murderous hellfire, when the shooting began.

The Cuban immediately threw himself to the pavement and rolled toward the sedan. Bullets burned air above his body. Slugs literally tugged at the loose cloth of his jacket. Two bullets creased his rib cage and split open flesh. Bone snapped as a projectile struck a rib.

Hot agony bolted through Encizo's left leg when a 7.62mm missile punched into his ankle, splintering bone. The Cuban rolled over the edge of the curb and slipped under the sedan. His leg felt as if it had been lanced by white-hot nails. Blood oozed from the wound in his side.

He tried to ignore the pain and reached for the Walther PPK holstered under his left armpit. In the cramped confines under the sedan, he did not have enough space to draw the pistol.

"Madre de Dios," Encizo growled through clenched teeth.

The metallic rattle of enemy guns continued. Encizo was trapped—his two Phoenix Force partners were still inside the sedan, Rachel had been exposed to the rain of bullets, but there was nothing he could do. He was trapped, helpless.

Gary Manning and Keio Ohara reacted to the ambush like the seasoned combat veterans they were. Ohara quickly climbed over the backrest and dropped into the back seat of the sedan. Keio was eager to get his hands on the collection of weapons stored there, and he also wanted to give the Canadian enough room to duck under the dashboard if the windshield began to give way under the onslaught of bullets.

The weaponry in the back seat consisted of two Uzi submachine guns, a Galil assault rifle and a box of hand grenades. The Japanese seized the Galil and slid it over the backrest to Manning. The Canadian took the Israeli-made auto-rifle and snapped back the bolt to chamber a round.

Manning waited until his partner armed himself with an Uzi. Ohara handed the Canadian two M-26 grenades.

"You handle the guys in the cab," Manning instructed. "I'll take care of the newsstand."

"Don't forget the men on the roof," Ohara said.

"I won't. Ready?"

Ohara nodded.

"Now!"

The pair moved in unison, throwing open the front and back doors on the passenger side of the sedan. Using the armor-plated doors for cover, the two warriors swung their weapons toward their targets and opened fire.

Manning blasted the newsstand with a ruthless volley of Galil slugs. The tiny pasteboard structure offered little protection from the high-velocity 5.56mm rounds. Magazines and newspapers flew from the racks and the front of the stand burst apart.

Two men stumbled onto the sidewalk. One lay motionless, blood gushing from a fatal wound.

The other scrambled upright and turned his PPSh 41 machine gun on the sedan. Manning hit him in the chest with a 3-round burst of Galil death. The terrorist seemed to be yanked backward by invisible cables. Then he crashed to the ground.

Ohara hosed the taxi cab with 9mm rounds. The windshield exploded. One of the gunmen inside the cab convulsed as bullets punched into his face and chest. The other terrorists ducked. There were still three left, two positioned at the side of the cab, a third inside the vehicle.

The Japanese quickly pulled the pin from an M-26 blaster and tossed the grenade at the cab. He aimed low, sending the M-26 to the edge of the curb beside the enemy vehicle.

One of the terrorists cried out in alarm and reached for the grenade, hoping to throw it back at the Phoenix Force defenders. He exposed himself to Ohara's field of fire. The Japanese nailed the guy with a burst of Uzi slugs. His corpse fell beside the grenade.

The M-26 exploded. The blast flipped the taxi onto its roof. The two United Arab terrorists who were perched beside the vehicle were blasted to the pavement. Both were dead.

The terrorist inside the cab had miraculously survived the grenade blast, although his right arm had been broken when the car flipped. He kicked open a door and crawled from the wreck. The terrorist pulled a 7.65mm Czech M1950 pistol from under his shirt and began to creep around the cab, trying to attack Ohara from a blind side.

The Japanese warrior failed to notice the new threat, but Rafael Encizo saw the terrorist's feet as the man approached. Still hidden under the belly of the car, Encizo carefully poked his head out to make sure the boots belonged to an enemy.

His suspicions confirmed, the Cuban wiggled out from under the sedan. Pain from his shattered ankle and cracked rib lanced through his body. He quickly yanked the Walther from leather and aimed from a prone stance.

Encizo triggered the PPK twice. Two .380 rounds tore into the terrorist's belly. The Arab doubled up in agony, blood spilling from his ravaged intestines. The Cuban fired again, splitting his opponent's skull with two well-placed bullets.

After wasting the two men stationed at the newsstand, Gary Manning directed his attention to the pair of terrorists on the rooftop across the street. Bullets ricocheted against the top of the sedan as the snipers continued to fire at the Phoenix Force defenders with a pair of AK-47 rifles.

The Canadian crouched by the hood of the car and carefully aimed his Galil rifle at the terrorist gunmen. He waited until one of the Arabs, preparing to fire, raised head, shoulders and Kalashnikov. Manning squeezed the trigger.

The terrorist screamed and dropped his Russian

assault rifle. The AK-47 clattered on the sidewalk below. The Arab grabbed his bullet-shattered face in both hands and sprawled on his belly.

The remaining terrorist glanced at the corpse of his partner. Aware that all his UAF comrades had been killed in the battle, he realized the mission was a failure. All that interested him was to escape with his life. He needed a distraction to buy a few precious seconds to flee.

The man pulled the pin from a Soviet F-1 hand grenade and rose to throw the minibomb. Manning spotted him and fired the Galil. Three 5.56mm slugs struck the terrorist in the upper chest. He fell onto the roof, the F-1 slipping from his fingers. Horrified, he stared at the grenade that rolled just beyond his reach.

The Soviet blaster exploded. The tattered remains of the two terrorists were blown onto the street in a ghastly shower.

Keio Ohara rushed to Encizo and knelt beside the wounded Cuban. He quickly examined the injured man. The Japanese ripped open Encizo's shirt and checked his partner's bullet-gouged rib cage. A glimpse of the splintered bone jutting from flesh at Encizo's ankle convinced Ohara not to touch it.

"How bad is it?" Gary Manning asked as he joined his teammates.

"We have to get him to a hospital," Ohara said.

"Rachel," Encizo rasped. "What happened to Rachel?"

"Take it easy," the Canadian said soothingly.

"Where is she?" Encizo demanded.

"I'm sorry, Rafael," Manning said. "Rachel's dead."

18

"How is he?" Yakov Katzenelenbogen asked when Gary Manning and Keio Ohara entered the office of the Mossad director.

"The wound in Rafael's side isn't serious," the Japanese answered. "A broken rib, slight tissue damage, that's all."

"His ankle is broken," Manning explained. "But the doctor said it isn't as bad as it looks. Thank God for that. It looked like his foot was about to fall off."

"It's a compound fracture," Ohara added. "Not a clean break, but the doctor is confident it will knit properly. Rafael will be out of action for at least a month or two."

"Considering the cross fire those terrorists hit you chaps with," McCarter remarked, "it was bloody lucky he wasn't chewed to pieces."

"That's what happened to Rachel," Manning said grimly. "Rafael is taking her death pretty hard."

"Too bad he won't be able to join us when we attack the Assassins' stronghold," Katz remarked.

Gary Manning's usual poker face and Ohara's

mask of perpetual calm vanished. They turned to Katz, eagerness displayed in their expressions.

"Have you found where it is?" the Canadian asked.

"Abdul Monsul was very cooperative," Katz said. "He awoke to find himself on a marble slab, surrounded by amazed Israelis. He was quite convinced that he had just returned from 'paradise' and that he should spill his guts to us."

"Our charade worked," Manning commented.

"It was quite successful," Major Nizam confirmed. "He told us everything he knew about Hassan and the Assassins."

"Yakov's theory was dead on target," McCarter added. "From the description Monsul gave us, the current leader of the Assassins had modeled himself after the original Hassan and he's using all the old tricks and a lot of new ones as well."

"Monsul has a good eye for detail," Katz declared. "His memory hasn't been totally damaged despite all those drugs he's been taking over the years. We've actually got a rough blueprint of the headquarters building. A large section of the place was off limits to most of Hassan's followers, but we've still got a good idea of what to expect when we hit the Assassins' lair."

"Where are the bastards?" Manning asked.

"In the Ish Al-Ghourab Mountains in the West Bank of Jordan," Katz answered.

"Israeli spy planes have been flying recon missions over that area for years," the Mossad director explained.

"What about the Assassins' lair?" Manning asked. "Do we have a fix on the site?"

"The recon film files were processed through a computer for the most likely area for the headquarters based on Monsul's descriptions. Heat sensors indicate there's a large well-populated fortress located between the peaks of four mountains at the Ish Al-Ghourab Range."

"Are you certain this isn't a covert Jordanian military base?" Ohara inquired.

"That's what we've always assumed it was in the past," the director replied. "But we have good reason to suspect this is the terrorist headquarters."

"We'd damn well better make sure before we launch an attack on the place," McCarter stated.

"You're talking about crossing the border into Jordan?" the head of Mossad said. "That would be considered an invasion by Israel. I thought you people wanted to prevent a war in the Middle East, not start one."

"Not to worry," Katz urged. "I've spoken with the prime minister and he's going to try to explain the situation to Jordan. He's probably on the hot line talking to Hussein at this very minute."

"King Hussein?" the director said, staring at Yakov.

"He can give us permission to cross the border," the colonel answered.

"He won't," the Mossad chief stated. "Jordan has refused to recognize Israel—it recognizes the goddamn Palestine Liberation Organization as the legitimate representative of the Palestinian people. Hussein can hardly be called a friend of Israel."

"He doesn't qualify as an enemy either," Major Nizam stated. "Jordan has one of the largest, best-trained and best-armed militaries in the Middle East, yet they haven't made an aggressive move against Israel for many years."

"Hussein is a bit unpredictable," Katz added. "But he hasn't allowed any anti-Israeli terrorist camps to be set up in his country since 1970."

The telephone on the director's desk rang. He picked up the receiver. The Mossad boss stiffened as he listened to the caller. At last he hung up.

"I owe you an apology, Colonel Katz," the director declared. "You were right about a double agent in Mossad."

"What happened?" Katz asked.

"That was Lieutenant Colonel Zavarj," the Director explained. "He just killed Major Eytan."

KATZENELENBOGEN STARED DOWN at the corpse of Major Uri Eytan. The man had been shot twice in the chest. Both bullets had pierced the heart. Next to the corpse lay a dagger.

Keio Ohara, who had accompanied Katz to Major Eytan's quarters, knelt beside the dead man and noticed that Eytan's sleeve was rolled up to the shoulder.

"There's a star-shaped tattoo on his deltoid," the Japanese declared. "Identical to the others found on members of the Assassin cult."

"Did you pull back his sleeve, Colonel Zavarj?" Katz inquired.

The Shremuth Modiin officer sat on a sofa with a glass of brandy in his hands. An Eagle .357 pistol was on the coffee table in front of him. Zavarj took a long swallow of brandy before he spoke.

"Yes, sir," he replied. "When I shot him in the chest he started to claw at his shoulder instead of the wound. I couldn't understand why until I checked and found that star."

"Why were you here in Eytan's apartment?" Katz asked.

"He invited me here," Zavarj explained. "The major said he wanted to talk to me about the assassination attempt. He and I were in charge of the prime minister's security at the hospital until that happened. We realized you suspected one of us was an enemy agent. Eytan claimed he had a way to prove we were innocent."

Zavarj took another gulp of brandy. Katz removed a pack of Camels and offered one to the intel officer.

"I've been trying to quit," Zavarj remarked, but he took a cigarette anyway.

"Try again tomorrow," Yakov advised. "Finish your story."

"Not much to tell," Zavarj said as he fired the cigarette. "I came here. Eytan poured me a drink and suddenly pulled that knife. I had to shoot him."

Katz glanced at the button-flap holster on Zavarj's hip. "You were lucky you managed to draw your gun in time, Colonel."

"I had the flap open," Zavarj stated. "You weren't the only person who was suspicious of Eytan, sir."

19

David McCarter wore a wolfish smile when he met Katz and Ohara at the office of the Mossad director. The Briton was dressed in a night-camouflage uniform with the pet Browning Hi-Power holstered under his left arm and the Ingram M-10 dangling from a shoulder strap. His belt was equipped with plenty of ammo pouches and an assortment of concussion and M-26 fragmentation grenades.

McCarter was ready to go to war. War against international terrorism.

"The prime minister called while you two were visiting Zavarj," McCarter explained. "He talked to Hussein. The king was a bit suspicious, but he checked with his prime minister—who is also the minister of defense in Jordan. The chap confirmed that they don't have any military stronghold in the Ish Al-Ghourab mountains."

"Did they have any information about what is there?" Ohara inquired.

"Yes," the Briton nodded. "The place is supposed to be a rather secluded mosque. Apparently the Jordanian minister of Islamic affairs had a file on it. The 'mosque' allegedly belongs to an obscure religious sect which is described as an offshoot of Ismailis Muslims.''

"I can see why that cover would make sense in Jordan,'' Katz remarked. "The country is almost ninety-five percent Sunni Moslem. They'd probably be quite pleased to have a different religious sect segregate itself to avoid confrontations between the two different faiths.''

"Well,'' McCarter continued. "The king said that he doesn't want war in the Middle East, and he's already forbidden terrorist camps from being set up in his country. So he also wants the Assassins put out of business.''

"The king obviously approved of our mission or you wouldn't be dressed for night combat,'' Ohara said.

"Yeah, but he still seems a trifle suspicious,'' the Briton said. "After all, it wouldn't look very good to the rest of the Arab world if he gave Israel permission to fly into Jordan to attack a genuine mosque.''

"He wants more proof?'' Katz asked.

"Not really,'' McCarter said, grinning. "See, the king has given permission for a recon mission to get more evidence. We can fly only one helicopter across the border with no more than twelve men on board.''

"And that's why you're so pleased?'' Katz asked. "You think we'll go in and raid the place anyway.''

"Why not?'' the Briton replied. "We'll find

the evidence to make the king happy and take care of the Assassins at the same time.''

Gary Manning approached from the end of the corridor beyond the office. He was also suited in combat black, with an Eagle .357 Magnum in a hip holster, a Galil rifle slung over his shoulder and a small black backpack strapped around the small of his back.

''I see you guys have been talking to 'rough and ready' McCarter,'' the Canadian remarked. ''What do you think of the mission, Katz?''

''I'd feel better about it if Rafael was here,'' the colonel replied. ''This job looks like it will be as tough as any we've had in the past and we're short one-fifth of our usual manpower.''

''The director has assured us we can have half a dozen Israeli commandos for the mission,'' Manning said.

''Members of the Independent Paratrooper Detachment?'' Katz inquired.

''Yeah,'' the Canadian replied. ''Specially trained for this sort of mission.''

''The two Egyptians also want to come along,'' McCarter added.

''Major Nizam and Captain Malik?'' the Phoenix Force commander said. ''I don't think they should.''

''They're trained commandos and antiterrorists,'' Manning said. ''And they insist that the fate of their country is also at stake.''

''They've got a point there,'' Katz agreed.

"Half a dozen Israeli soldiers, the two Egyptians and the four of us," Ohara mused. "That's twelve."

"The desperate dozen," McCarter said.

"An apt title," Katz said. "All right, meet with the rest of the volunteers and screen them as best you can. Make certain we don't have any crazy-brave lunatics in the crowd. We need professionals, not zealots who think it will be a lot of fun to kick the hell out of a nest of Arab terrorists."

"Does that mean we can't take David with us?" the Canadian asked.

"Leap up my ass," McCarter shot at Manning. The pair laughed.

"You've all had more time than I to study the Israeli recon photos," Keio Ohara stated. "What would you guess the stronghold's security is like?"

"It has the potential to be very good," Manning answered. "Mountains all around it. They probably chose the site because the peaks conceal their exact position. It offers some protection, as well, and a good site for sentries."

"Do you think they have radar?" Ohara asked.

"It doesn't really matter if they do or not. We can't land a chopper among those mountain peaks anyway," McCarter said.

"We'll have to land a few miles from the range," Manning agreed, "and hoof it from there. Our main problems will be sentries, surveillance cameras and maybe a LSW system.''

"Forget about a Land Sonar Wave," Ohara commented. "It would be useless in the middle of so many mountain peaks and boulders."

"What about heat sensors?" Katz asked. "They might not function well in the desert during the day, but at night the temperature drops dramatically. Human body heat could be detected then."

"Any way we can neutralize something like that?" Manning asked Ohara.

"Not unless we know what sort of system they might have," the Japanese electronics wizard replied. "Security devices aren't the biggest problem," Ohara remarked. "The main concern is the Assassins themselves."

"Keio's right," Katz agreed. "They're absolute fanatics who don't have much fear of death. Such zealots may be willing to destroy the entire fortress themselves simply to kill some infidels and free their souls from earthly chains."

"Great," Manning growled. "Still looking forward to this mission, David?"

"Risk is what makes life interesting, mate."

"Colonel Katzenelenbogen?" a young man dressed in the fatigue uniform and red beret of an Israeli paratrooper called to Yakov. "I'm Captain Rosen, senior officer of the volunteer group for the mission, sir."

"Rosen?" Katz raised an eyebrow. "You were with hospital security when the assassins first tried to kill the prime minister, correct?"

"Yes, sir," Rosen admitted. "I was with the group commanded by Major Eytan. I hope that doesn't disqualify me, Colonel."

"Certainly not," Yakov assured him. "Get your men together for a briefing. We want to get on with the mission as soon as possible."

"Yes, sir." The captain saluted. "Oh, Colonel. Dr. Ben-David told me they've just identified several of the terrorists who ambushed your men earlier this evening."

"Anything special about them?" Katz asked.

"Well, none of them were Egyptians or Israeli Arabs," the captain answered. "They were Syrians and Libyans. All have records of association with the United Arab Front."

"That's Nasser Fawzi's outfit," Katz declared. "One of the worst terrorist gangs in the Middle East."

"You figure the UAF hired the Assassins?" McCarter asked.

"Seems likely," Yakov answered. "Fawzi's group is too small to do much on their own, but they're certainly radical enough to try and start a war."

"Hassan wouldn't sell his services cheaply," Manning mused. "How could the UAF afford him?"

"Who's paying the bills doesn't matter," McCarter shrugged. "All we have to deal with is the terrorists themselves."

"You make it sound easy," Captain Rosen said.

"It won't be easy," the Briton stated. "But it really isn't complicated either—it's kill or be killed."

20

The UH-1 Huey transport helicopter crossed the border into Jordan at 0312. An Israeli paratrooper was at the controls.

Colonel Katzenelenbogen addressed the assault team at the back of the gunship cabin.

"Gentlemen," he said, "we'll soon be arriving at our destination. If you have any questions, let's hear them now."

"Do we take prisoners?" Staff Sergeant Mosshin, an Israeli paratrooper, asked.

"That will be up to the terrorists," Katz replied. "We're not murderers. If a man surrenders, we'll take him alive. But don't count on any of these characters giving up. The Assassins are religious fanatics who can hardly wait to die for Allah. No offense to our two Muslim friends from Egypt."

"No offense taken, Colonel," Major Nizam assured him. "Lunatics such as the Assassins are not typical of the Islamic religion. Their faith is an insult to any true Muslim."

"Some of you are familiar with the United Arab Front," Katz continued. "They've got a reputation for being vicious, ruthless and brutal.

The UAF members who might be at the stronghold are just as dangerous as the Assassins.''

"Don't think because a bloke comes at you without a gun that he's not a genuine threat," McCarter warned.

"The Assassins' daggers are coated with poison—one scratch can be lethal.''

"Sir?'' a young lieutenant named Halpern said. "Why are we going in after these Arabs? Why not just bomb the place and blow them all to hell?''

"Because we have to get evidence to prove this raid was justified,'' Katz replied. "We don't want Israel to be accused of an unjust invasion into Jordan.''

"Besides,'' Ohara added, "the Jordanians have allowed us to legally enter their country. They deserve some proof to confirm that their faith was justified.''

"A good point, Keio,'' Yakov agreed. "The Jordanians are cooperating with us. So are our two Egyptian friends who are also risking their lives to help prevent a war in the Middle East.''

"We're glad to be here, Colonel,'' Captain Malik told him.

"Israelis and Arabs have joined forces against a common enemy,'' Katz declared. "That's another reason why this mission has to succeed. The rest of the world will probably never know about tonight, but the governments of Israel, Egypt and Jordan will be aware of what happened. These three nations are trusting each other. We have to make certain none of them has reason to regret that trust."

"Might even start a trend," Manning remarked.

"We can hope so," Katz said. "Any more questions?"

There were none. Yakov returned to his seat next to Captain Rosen. The young officer checked his supply of banana clips for a Galil rifle to be certain all the magazines were fully loaded.

"Mind if I ask you a question, Captain?" Katz asked.

"About the day the Assassins attempted to kill the prime minister?" Rosen guessed.

"Yes. Did you know the terrorists had attacked a decoy and the prime minister was actually located in a different room?"

"Yes, sir," Rosen nodded. "I was with the squad commanded by Mossad. We knew about the decoy, but the Sherith Modiin team didn't. I imagine military intelligence was pretty upset when they found out they'd been lied to by Mossad, but it had to be done to be sure the guards on the decoy section would be convincing."

"I understand," Katz assured him.

"Something I'm curious about, Colonel," Rosen said. "I saw Major Eytan's corpse carried into Doctor Ben-David's office. Do you know why?"

"I ordered an autopsy," Katz answered. "It

should be completed by the time we return to Tel Aviv.''

David McCarter checked the firing mechanism of a Barnett Commando crossbow. It featured several modern innovations to the original design of a weapon created centuries ago. The Barnett had a skeletal metal stock and a cocking lever.

"Going to play William Tell?" Manning asked with a grin.

"I'll have you know we've been using these Commando crossbows for years in the SAS," McCarter replied as he inspected the weapon's bolts. "It has a longer, more accurate range than most rifles and it makes less noise than a firearm with a sound suppressor. No muzzle-flash to worry about either. Ideal for taking out a sentry at night."

"The problem with an arrow," the Canadian said, "is it doesn't have as much knock-down force as a bullet."

"That's why I've added an extra ingredient to these crossbow bolts," McCarter explained. "I split the shaft of each bolt near the tip and added about twenty cubic centimeters of cyanide."

"I thought you British believed in being sporting," Manning said.

"We British believe in survival."

AT 0330, the Huey gunship landed on a desert on the West Bank of Jordan, eight miles from the Ish Al-Ghourab Mountains. The twelve-man strike force left the chopper and began to march toward their objective.

The desert was cold, barren. An occasional gnarled tree or a dry gulch, which had once been a stream, broke the monotony of the featureless terrain.

The desert sky was magnificent. Undisturbed by city lights or smog, it was a panorama of stars set against a field of dark velvet. In the horizon lurked the Ish Al-Ghourab Mountains.

Every member of the team was well armed. Most carried Galil assault rifles or Uzi machine guns, side arms and an assortment of grenades, knives and garrotes. Three Israelis also carried bazookalike LAW rocket launchers. Two others had medical kits on their backs, and one brought a field radio to contact the commander of a Jordanian Yarmuk company that was somewhere in the desert, watching the area through infrared telescopes.

Katz and Ohara, like McCarter and Manning, had also armed themselves to the teeth. In addition to his Uzi subgun, Katz wore an Eagle pistol in shoulder leather. The ambidextrous safety feature appealed to the one-handed Israeli. He also carried his standard side arm, a .45-caliber Colt Commander, in a hip holster.

Keio Ohara had chosen an M-16 with a 203 grenade launcher attached to the barrel. He also had a 1911A1 Colt automatic and a *kusarigama*—an ancient samurai weapon consisting of an eight-foot chain with a *kama*—fighting sickle—

attached to one end and a steel ball to the other. The rest of the members of the team wondered why Ohara had chosen such an odd weapon, but no one asked him about the *kusarigama*. The Japanese had to have had a reason for his selection.

"David and Keio will take the point," Katz declared as he screwed a foot-long silencer to the threaded barrel of his Uzi.

"Everyone keep your eyes open for sentries and surveillance cameras," Manning added, checking the infrared scope on his Galil.

Phoenix Force and its allies continued toward the mountains—toward a deadly confrontation with the Order of the Assassins.

21

Four white-robed figures, armed with AK-47 assault rifles, stood sentry duty on the mountain peaks surrounding the fortress. They scanned the area, determined to protect their master's palace.

The Assassin sentries used a powerful stimulant to assure they did not surrender to fatigue. The drug, however, also caused a euphoria that dulled their senses.

Something sizzled through the dark sky. Metal and wood slapped into flesh. A sentry stiffened and dropped his rifle. His mouth opened in a silent scream that died in his throat as poison pumped within his punctured heart.

The other sentries saw their comrade collapse. A short feathered shaft jutted from the center of his chest. An Assassin guard gasped and unslung his Kalashnikov, unaware that the cross hairs of an infrared scope bisected his face.

Gary Manning squeezed the trigger of his Galil. The silencer attached to the Israeli rifle coughed harshly. A 5.56mm bullet smashed into the guard's forehead, slicing through his brain like an ice pick through paper.

The remaining sentries turned toward the muffled report of Manning's weapon. Desperately they tried to locate the invisible assailant. Something whistled through the air. A long metal tentacle struck out from the darkness.

An Assassin glimpsed the whirling *kama* at the end of the chain that hurled toward his head. Steel links circled his neck. Sharp metal bit into flesh.

Keio Ohara forcibly yanked the *kusarigama*. The sickle blade ripped out the sentry's throat. The guard crumbled against the rock wall, blood spilling from the terrible wound.

The remaining sentry heard the gurgle of blood that gushed from his slain partner's throat. David McCarter aimed his Barnett crossbow and squeezed the trigger to release the taut bowstring. A bolt hissed through the air and slammed into the Assassin's back.

The sharp tip pierced flesh under the terrorist's left shoulder blade and pierced the man's heart. His body convulsed wildly as cyanide burned through his bloodstream. The sentry plunged over the edge of the cliff. He was dead before his body crashed to earth hundreds of feet below.

McCarter worked the cocking lever of the crossbow to load another bolt into the grooved frame.

"I haven't found any cameras or microphones," Keio Ohara said as he gathered up his *kusarigama*.

"Looks like Hassan doesn't feel he needs any sophisticated security devices," Lieutenant Halpern remarked as he and Katzenelenbogen joined the other members of Phoenix Force.

"Maybe," Yakov replied. "But don't assume anything."

"By the Prophet," Major Nizam whispered as he stared at the building below. "This would impress Pharaoh Khufu himself."

The Assassin stronghold, located in a crevasse between the mountain peaks, was an incredible stone structure that covered an area of almost two city blocks. Only one story high, the building seemed taller because it was capped by a huge decorative dome and a pointed cupola. Two *manaras*—prayer towers—flanked both sides of the main door at the face of the structure.

"McCarter," Katz said, "take Nizam, Malik, Captain Rosen and one of the other Israelis. Move to the rear of the palace and check for sentries, cameras, emergency exits and that sort of thing."

The Briton nodded and quickly assembled his team. McCarter's group descended to the stronghold, while Katz gathered the rest of the men to prepare the assault.

"Only seems to be one entrance at the front," Manning declared as he scanned the area through the infrared scope on his rifle. "There are steel bars on the windows."

The Canadian's gaze traveled to the rock walls of the stronghold, which McCarter's team was approaching. He suddenly noticed a tiny circle of light among the stones. Above the light jutted the snout of a machine gun, mounted on a pedestal.

"Shit," Manning gasped. "They've got trap guns set up."

"What kind?" Katz asked tensely.

"Looks like a PPS machine gun mounted on a robot system with an electronic eye," the Canadian replied. "If one of our men breaks the light beam...."

One of the trap guns suddenly exploded with a volley of full-auto fire. An Israeli soldier in McCarter's group screamed as five 7.62mm slugs ripped into his torso. The paratrooper fell in a bloodied heap, while the rest of the team dived for cover. The machine gun revolved on its pedestal and continued to spit bullets at the commandos.

"Get those rockets ready," Katz shouted. "Keio, the grenade launcher."

The Japanese warrior had already loaded an HE cartridge grenade into the breech of his 203 launcher. He aimed the weapon at the automated machine gun below and triggered the 203. The grenade blasted the robot gun to bits.

"Hit the door," Katz ordered. "Blow it apart. We're going in hard."

Sergeant Mosshin fired a LAW. The rocket sizzled across the sky like a bolt of vengeful lightning. The front of the building erupted in a supernova of yellow light. The entrance crumbled from the blast.

"Watch for trap guns," Manning warned as he prepared to charge. "Take them out with grenades."

David McCarter knew what had happened the second the robot machine gun opened fire. He also knew that any further attempt at stealth would be useless. The Briton left the Barnett crossbow on the ground and unslung his M-10 Ingram as white-robed figures began to pour out of the enemy stronghold.

"On your feet, men," he ordered. "Get to the back door. I'll cover you. And watch out for those bloody booby traps."

The Englishman rose and opened fire on the Assassins. Two terrorists were kicked into death before they even realized where the shots were coming from. Others swung their Soviet-made weapons toward the Briton.

Full-auto fire snarled as the second wave of the assault force charged. Bullets cut down terrorists like a scythe sweeping in a wheat field. Blood splashed white uniforms and Assassins dropped lifelessly.

Major Nizam, Captain Rosen and Captain Malik dashed to the back of the building. Five Assassins were already in position there. The terrorists opened fire. Malik screamed as bullets crashed into his chest. The Egyptian fell.

Major Nizam and Captain Rosen immediately avenged their slain comrade. Their Uzi submachine guns blasted the Assassins. The killers shrieked as 9mm projectiles punched into flesh and pulverized faces. Those terrorists collapsed, but more appeared in the doorway of the building's back exit.

Nizam hosed the fanatics with Uzi slugs, while Captain Rosen yanked the pin from a M-26 hand grenade and tossed it through the doorway. Rosen grabbed Nizam and pulled him to the ground. The grenade exploded, spewing torn bits of terrorist bodies.

Phoenix Force burst through the main entrance. Assassins rushed into the assembly hall to confront the invaders, some armed only with their poison daggers.

The bastards with firearms let loose. Sergeant Mosshin's head recoiled violently as an AK-47 round smashed into the side of his skull.

Katzenelenbogen exhausted the ammunition from his Uzi, sending three Assassins to hell. Before he could reload, a knife-wielding terrorist lunged at him. The Israeli colonel raised his empty submachine gun, blocking his opponent's knife with the Uzi's frame.

The Assassin clawed at the Uzi, ripping it from Katz's grasp. The Phoenix Force commander jumped back and swiftly drew the Colt .45 from its hip holster. The terrorist attacked again, thrusting his poison dagger at the Israeli's chest.

Yakov's prosthetic arm swooped forward. The steel hooks clamped around the man's wrist. The startled Assassin screamed as the powerful hooks crushed bone and forced him to drop the knife.

Katz jammed the muzzle of his Colt Commander under the terrorist's ribs and squeezed the trigger. A 185-grain bullet burned into vital organs. Katz released the dying man, then fired another .45 slug into his chest to end his suffering.

Keio Ohara's M-16 jammed. He ducked behind a stone pillar, yanked the magazine out of the rifle and pulled back the bolt to eject a warped cartridge casing from the breech. Three Assassins found him and attacked.

Ohara quickly discarded the empty M-16 and unslung the *kusarigama* from his shoulder. The Japanese whirled the chain weapon in a fast figure-eight pattern that held the aggressors at bay.

Ohara executed a deft snap of the wrist. The sickle blade swung upward and struck flesh. An Assassin screamed and staggered backward, the steel *kama* blade buried deep in his chest.

Another terrorist lunged forward as Ohara tore the blade from the dead man's chest. Ohara swung the other end of his *kusarigama*. The steel ball whistled through air, then crashed into the side of the man's skull, crushing his head.

The third Assassin dived forward with a wild knife thrust. Ohara nimbly dodged the poison blade and flipped the length of chain around the killer's wrist, pulling the chain taunt, the steel links gripped the man's wrist like a vise and rendered his knife useless.

Ohara lashed out, kicking his opponent in the testicles. The terrorist gasped and doubled up in agony. The Japanese warrior grabbed him by the hair, yanked his head back and slashed a shuto stroke with his other hand. The side of his palm crushed his opponent's windpipe.

A scream of agony stole Ohara's attention. He turned sharply and saw a large, muscular black man standing over an Israeli paratrooper with a scimiter in his fists. Blood dripped from the blade of the sword.

Jemal saw Ohara at the same instant. A loud moan escaped from Jemal's throat. He charged— the scimitar held overhead in a two- fisted grip— before Ohara could gather up his *kusarigma*.

The Japanese martial artist waited for the sword-wielding adversary to close in. Then Ohara stepped forward and raised his arms, slamming the heels of both palms into Jemal's forearms, checking the sword stroke before the Assassin manservant could bring his weapon to play.

Ohara immediately delivered a snap-kick between Jemal's splayed legs. The eunuch merely smiled. The Phoenix Force martial-arts champ was stunned by Jemal's casual response to a blow that would have paralyzed most men.

The eunuch attacked. He brought the pommel of his sword down hard between the Oriental's shoulder blades. Ohara bent over from the blow.

Jemal promptly smashed a knee into his jaw-bone.

The Phoenix Force fighter hit the floor, the back of his head striking the stone surface. He gazed up through a foggy curtain as Jemal raised the sword high. A black veil of unconsciousness dropped over Ohara.

22

David McCarter had used all thirty-two rounds of ammo from his M-10 during the battle. He was about to reload when he saw Keio Ohara fall. The Briton instantly drew his Browning Hi-Power from shoulder leather.

Snap aiming, the British pistol champ fired a hasty shot at the sword-swinging killer, who was about to split Ohara into halves with his scimitar. Sparks flew when the 115-grain 9mm bullet struck the blade of Jemal's sword. The black man staggered and fell, the scimitar slipping from his grasp.

McCarter rushed forward, prepared to put a bullet into Jemal's brain to make certain he stayed down forever. The Briton stopped for a second when he heard Ohara groan. McCarter glanced down at his partner, relieved Ohara was still alive.

Jemal shot up from the floor.

He grabbed McCarter's arm and pulled hard. The Briton stumbled into a stone pillar. The sudden impact jarred the Browning from his hand. McCarter whirled to face Jemal. The eunuch lunged forward, hands aimed at the Phoenix Force commando's throat.

McCarter ducked under the manservant's hands and caught Jemal on the side of the jaw with a solid left hook, followed by a right cross. His knuckles stung from the impact of the punches, yet Jemal's head barely moved from the blows.

"Shit," the Briton rasped as the eunuch charged once more.

The Englishman avoided Jemal's groping fingers by stepping to the side. He rammed a fist into the brute's kidney and slashed the side of his hand into the base of Jemal's skull. The muscular servant responded by lashing a forearm into McCarter's chest.

McCarter felt as if he had been hit with a baseball. The blow knocked him off his feet. His back smacked against the floor hard. The Briton gazed up to see Jemal lunge toward him, still determined to throttle the life from his adversary.

"Bloody hell," the stubborn Phoenix warrior growled.

He quickly raised a leg and slammed the bottom of his boot into the eunuch's face. The kick crushed cartilage in Jemal's nose and cracked the philtrum bone in his upper jaw. The Assassin flunky staggered backward, dazed by the blow.

McCarter did not try to rise from the floor. He braced himself with his hands and lashed out with both legs. His left foot hooked Jemal's ankle and his right stomped into the man's knee—a simple jujitsu technique McCarter had learned in the SAS. It worked beautifully. Jemal crashed to the floor, pain riding up his leg from the dislocated kneecap.

The Briton scrambled across the floor to the discarded scimitar. Jemal tried to rise, but his damaged leg buckled and he dropped to his knees. The brute glanced up as McCarter charged forward. He opened his mouth in a silent scream when he saw the Briton swing the sword in a powerful stroke.

The ugly thud of sharp metal striking flesh filled McCarter's ears. Blood spurted across the Briton's shirt. Jemal's severed head tumbled across the floor.

McCarter tossed the blood-stained scimitar aside and gathered up his Browning. Keio Ohara groaned and sat up, rubbing his sore jaw and shaking his head.

"Don't lie about, mate," McCarter said crisply. "Still work to be done."

Gary Manning fitted four ounces of C-4 into the crack of a door at the opposite side of the assembly hall. He inserted a pencil detonator into the white puttylike substance, then ducked behind a pillar, where Colonel Katzenelenbogen was already stationed. Twenty second later the C-4 exploded.

The blast tore apart the door and destroyed a portion of the wall. Katz pulled the pin from a concussion grenade and hurled it through the opening. Another explosion erupted in the room beyond.

Katz and Manning dashed to the ragged hole

in the wall. Corpses of slain terrorists littered the floor. Three dazed figures were on their knees at the opposite side of the room. Instead of the white Assassin outfit, the trio wore green uniforms with checkered *keffiyeh* on their heads. Blood oozed from their nostrils and ears.

Wounded or not, the terrorists were still armed and dangerous. Manning sprayed them with Galil slugs. Their bodies tumbled backward into a wall.

"A lot of these guys aren't wearing white," the Canadian commented.

"White and red are the traditional colors of the Order of the Assassins," Katz explained. "The rest of these men must be members of the United Arab Front. Hassan had to keep them a secret from the rest of the cult in order to continue his charade as a religious leader."

"Well, this room is trashed," Manning commented. "Shall we see what's behind door number three?"

"Is it safe to blast the door lock in such close quarters?" Katz asked the Phoenix Force demolitions expert.

"I'll use a potassium-chlorate compound instead of C-4," Manning explained as he slipped off his backpack.

He removed a packet of gray gelatin and molded it to the doorframe while Katz stood guard. A pencil detonator triggered the explosive. The blast was mild.

However, an extremely violent explosion immediately followed. The wall burst and large chunks were shot across the room. Katz and Manning dived to the floor as the debris fell around them.

A piece of the wall, the size of a man's fist, struck Manning in the back of the skull. The Canadian slumped unconscious. Katz scrambled over to him and checked his pulse. The Israeli sighed with relief when he felt the strong throbbing artery in Manning's neck.

"Booby trap," Katz said through clenched teeth. "The bastards had the door rigged with explosives."

"Drop your gun," a voice demanded in Arabic.

Katz turned to see Colonel Nasser Fawzi stepping into the room. The Israeli left his Uzi on the floor and rose slowly with his arms held high. Fawzi kept a Makarov pistol aimed at Katz's chest as he drew closer.

"Katzenelenbogen," the terrorist said, smiling when he noticed the steel hooks at the end of Yakov's prosthetic arm. "I feel like we've hated each other for years. Now we finally meet."

"You must be Fawzi," Katz replied. "You're not living up to your reputation. You didn't shoot me in the back when you had the chance."

"I can kill you right here and now," the terrorist colonel declared. "But you're more useful to me alive."

"You think you can use me as a hostage to get out of here?" Katz shook his head. "It won't work. You'd do better to take your chances in court.''

"Don't be absurd, Katzenelenbogen." Fawzi sneered. "Unbuckle that gun belt.''

"What happened to Hassan?" Katz asked as he unfastened the web belt and dropped his holstered Colt Commander to the floor.

"He's in the other room," Fawzi replied. "In his private chamber where he lived like a king. I thought it would be an appropriate place for him to die.''

"You killed him?''

"My only regret is that I had to make it quick," Fawzi declared. "That idiot failed in his mission and got me and my comrades boxed in here when you attacked this place. A bullet in the back of the head was a far better fate than he deserved.''

"That's one way to dissolve a partnership." Katz shrugged.

"You have a gun in a holster under your arm," the terrorist said. "Take it out slowly and drop it on the floor.''

Yakov reached for the Eagle with his left hand.

"Not that way," Fawzi snapped. "Use the hook.''

"This prosthetic is a bit clumsy," Katz said. "I'm not certain I can. . . .''

"Do it, Jew!" the terrorist insisted. "It will be amusing to watch you. If I get bored I'll simply shoot off your other hand.''

"I'll try," Katz said as he awkwardly moved the hooks to the .357 under his arm.

"I'm getting impatient, cripple," Fawzi warned.

"Using me for a hostage won't work," Yakov told him as he shoved a hook against the safety catch of the Eagle pistol.

"If it doesn't," Fawzi said with a smile, "you'll die first, Jew."

"Your threats don't worry me," Katz remarked, clamping the prosthetic around the butt of the gun. "You tend to make too many mistakes."

"Shut up and get that gun out of the holster," the terrorist demanded.

Katzenelenbogen suddenly thrust his right arm forward. The Eagle pistol was held firmly in the artificial hand. A steel hook pulled the trigger before the startled terrorist colonel could react.

A 130-grain semijacketed hollowpoint slug blasted a hole between Fawzi's eyes. His head snapped back, blood and brains vomiting from his shattered skull. Nasser Fawzi crashed to the floor.

"That," Katz said as he pried the Eagle from the steel hooks and snapped on the safety catch, "was your last mistake."

"Colonel," a voice called from the doorway where Fawzi had appeared.

Katz turned sharply, the .357 automatic in his left fist. Major Nizam and Captain Rosen held up their empty hands in mock surrender. Yakov holstered his pistol as the pair approached.

"We found an office complete with filing cabinets and a computer with dozens of floppy disks," Rosen explained.

"The Captain is familiar with computer operations," Nizam declared. "He fed a couple of disks into the machine while I checked the files."

"We've got all the evidence we need, Colonel," Rosen said. "The location and structure of a 'garden paradise' used to brainwash personnel, a list of estimated costs for narcotics, weapons and even a holograph system."

"And we discovered that just from a very quick search," the Egyptian officer added.

"God," Gary Manning muttered as he sat up, massaging the back of his skull. "What happened?"

"Mission accomplished," Katz told him. "Go back to sleep."

23

Rafael Encizo entered the interrogation room. His lower leg was encased in a plaster cast, and he leaned heavily on a pair of crutches. Colonel Katzenelenbogen waited for the Cuban to close the door.

"Glad to see you're up and about, Rafael," Katz told him.

"I'm getting by," Encizo replied.

The Cuban glared at the chalk-white face of Lieutenant Colonel Ezra Zavarj who sat on a stool in the center of the room. Katz pointed his Eagle .357 at the Israeli military-intelligence officer's head.

"So this is the one," Encizo whispered, his voice a cold chill from a graveyard.

"You're wrong about me, Colonel," Zavarj insisted, sweat beads forming on his forehead.

"Captain Rosen told me that Major Eytan, being a Mossad officer, was aware that the prime minister was not in the hospital room which the Assassins attacked when they first tried to kill him," Katz said. "But you, being a Sheruth Modiin officer, did not know you were guarding a decoy. Now, why would the Assassins have attacked that room if they knew there was only a mannequin inside?''

"Maybe Eytan tried to convince his terrorist boss that he was on their side, but he still didn't want to actually assassinate the prime minister,'' Zavarj suggested.

"That's a pretty stupid theory,'' Encizo remarked.

"How do I know what his motives may have been?'' Zavarj snapped. "This is insane. You saw the star-shaped tattoo on Eytan's shoulder....''

"It wasn't a tattoo,'' Yakov stated. "The autopsy confirmed that it was only a skin decal. That was stupid to put that star on his shoulder, Zavarj. None of the Assassins wore their mark on such an obvious part of their body. A spy certainly wouldn't have the tattoo at all. That's as abserd as a KGB agent with a hammer and sickle on his forearm.''

"But you said the Assassins were religious fanatics,'' Zavarj replied.

"Yes. But they weren't that sloppy,'' Katz said. "They were, however, addicted to a variety of drugs. The autopsy found no traces of hashish or other narcotics in Major Eytan's body. However, when your quarters were searched, a hash pipe, synthetic heroin tablets and an assortment of other pills were discovered.

"We also found an Interarms bolt-action rifle,'' he continued. "Complete with a Bushnell telescopic scope and five .300 Winchester Magnum cartridges with explosive mercury-core slugs—suitable equipment for an assassination. You would have had plenty of opportunities to shoot the prime minister from a window after you framed Eytan as the spy and murdered him.''

"Colonel, I'm not . . . " Zavarj pleaded.

"It's finished," Yakov told him. "The Assassin cult has been crushed. The prime minister is still alive. Israel's relations with Egypt *and* Jordan have been strengthened by this business. You've failed in your mission, Zavarj. It's finished."

"What will they do with me?" Zavarj asked quietly.

"You should be familiar with Israeli law," Katz shrugged. "There's no doubt you'll be found guilty of espionage against the State of Israel. You'll either be executed or spend the rest of your life in prison. Probably the latter. An execution would mean some degree of publicity and the government, not to mention the Sheruth Modiin, would rather have a nice, quiet, top-secret trial and then plant you in a maximum security cell. You'll never see another human being who isn't wearing a prison-guard uniform."

"Do I have an alternative?" Zavarj asked.

"If you want it." Katz tilted his head toward Encizo.

Zavarj nodded in reply.

"He's all yours, Rafael," Katz said. "Make it clean and quick."

"I will," Encizo assured him. "How are the others, Katz?"

"McCarter came out of it without a scratch," Yakov said. "Gary's going to have a nasty lump on his head for a while, but nothing serious. Keio's only real injury is a wounded ego because he was knocked unconscious by a fellow Mc-Carter defeated in a hand-to-hand battle. That was a blow to his pride."

"Rachel would be pleased with how this mission ended," Encizo remarked sadly. "Katz, I know you don't approve of killing in cold blood...."

"An execution isn't murder," Yakov told him. "Zavarj himself approves of it. Don't you, Zavarj?"

"Get it over with," the former spy muttered tensely.

"What about the other members of Phoenix Force?" Encizo asked.

"We all agreed you should be the one to handle this," Yakov said. "It won't bring Rachel back, but it will help her rest in peace—at least in your heart."

"Thank you, Yakov," Encizo said.

Colonel Katzenelenbogen left the room as Encizo drew his silencer-equipped Walther PPK. Katz stepped into the corridor, closed the door and waited.

The Gar Wilson Forum

On October 23, 1983, a truck bomb driven by a terrorist crashed into the U.S. Marine compound in Lebanon and exploded. Two hundred forty-one American servicemen were killed. Colonel Geraghty, commander of our Marine forces in Lebanon, admitted that he'd ordered his troops *not* to load their M-16 rifles, in order to "preclude accidental discharge and possible injury to innocent civilians." On December 27, 1983, President Reagan accepted personal responsibility for any breach of security practices that allowed this incident. He claimed, "Local commanders on the ground have suffered quite enough."

However, total blame does not lie with the President or local commanders, because the Marines were following a procedure that has been SOP with U.S. military for over a decade. In the 1970s, during the height of the Baader-Meinhof and Black September terrorism in West Germany, American Army bases were still guarded by troops with unloaded rifles. Often sentries were not even issued ammunition, as you can read in Phoenix Force #9: *Ultimate Terror* (written before the Marine massacre in Lebanon).

Concern about firearm accidents or appearances for the sake of nervous civilians should not be allowed to endanger the lives of our servicemen or jeopardize military security.

Fatalities by firearm accidents are actually quite rare. Deaths caused by automobile accidents, electrical mishaps, falls and even food suffocation are more common.

Most civilians surely understand that soldiers must be armed to be effective. If our military personnel are unable to defend themselves, how can they be expected to protect our national security interests?

Gar

PHOENIX FORCE

#12 The Black Alchemists

MORE GREAT ACTION COMING SOON!

A rash of grisly murders and mutilations occur when packaged products all over the U.S. are contaminated with poisons, acids and other fiendish substances. A young woman applies face cream and her skin is shredded by ground glass and hydrochloric acid mixed in with the cream. An old man is blinded from acid in his eyedrop solution. . . .

Phoenix Force is joined by new member Calvin James to crack a network of horror that has the whole nation in its grip.

The fight with the Black Alchemists is so savage that one of the Phoenix Force warriors whispers his last words: "It is the best way for men like us, yes? It is good to die with friends."

Watch for new Phoenix Force titles wherever paperbacks are sold.

DON PENDLETON'S EXECUTIONER
MACK BOLAN

Sergeant Mercy in Nam... The Executioner in the Mafia Wars... Colonel John Phoenix in the Terrorist Wars.... Now Mack Bolan fights his loneliest war! You've never read writing like this before. Faceless dogsoldiers have killed April Rose. The Executioner's one link with compassion is broken. His path is clear: by fire and maneuver, he will rack up hell in a world shock-tilted by terror. Bolan wages unsanctioned war—everywhere!

GOLD EAGLE

Available wherever paperbacks are sold.

AVAILABLE NOW!
New from Gold Eagle Books

TRACK

#1 The Ninety-Nine
#2 Atrocity

Dan Track learned how to fight by growing up
orphaned among southside Chicago gangs. Famous in
the U.S. Army for his genius-level IQ and brawny
mastery of survival, he now pursues a man who is the
shadow of death itself, a zealot whose mad dream is
everybody's worst nightmare. Only Track stands
between us and nuclear hell! This is the explosive new
series by Jerry Ahern, world-renowned author of
The Survivalist.

Countdown to the end of the goddamned world,
thought Daniel Track. Somewhere on the train
there's a five-hundred-kiloton nuclear bomb set to go
off in the middle of downtown Chicago.

An evil madman called Johannes Kreiger, kill-hard
leader of a die-hard Nazi underground, has
masterminded the theft of one hundred of these
U.S.-made nuclear warheads. Chicago is his first
stop on a twisted dream-ride to global nuclear
perdition.

Track has fifteen minutes to defuse the deadly device.
Fifteen minutes to cancel Kreiger's ticket. Fifteen
minutes to make it one down and ninety-nine to go!

Available wherever paperbacks are sold.

Mack Bolan's
PHOENIX FORCE
by Gar Wilson

Schooled in guerilla warfare, equipped with all the
latest lethal hardware, Phoenix Force battles the powers
of darkness in an endless crusade for freedom, justice
and the rights of the individual. Follow the adventures
of one of the legends of the genre. Phoenix Force is the
free world's foreign legion!

"Gar Wilson is excellent! Raw action attacks the reader
on every page."

—Don Pendleton

Phoenix Force titles are available
wherever paperbacks are sold.

GOLD
EAGLE

JOIN FORCES WITH MACK BOLAN AND HIS NEW COMBAT TEAMS!

FREE! MACK BOLAN BUMPER STICKER

"LIVE LARGE" Mack Bolan

GOLD EAGLE BOOKS

E'S EXPLOSIVE.
E'S UNSTOPPABLE.
E'S MACK BOLAN!

learned his deadly skills in Vietnam…then put them to good use by
troying the Mafia in a blazing one-man war. Now **Mack Bolan** ventures
her into the cold to take on his deadliest challenge yet—the KGB's
rldwide terror machine.

Follow the lone warrior on his exciting new missions…and get ready for
re nonstop action from his high-powered combat teams: **Able Team**—
an's famous Death Squad—battling urban savagery too brutal and volatile for
ular law enforcement. And **Phoenix Force**—five extraordinary warriors
dpicked by Bolan to fight the dirtiest of antiterrorist wars, blazing into even
ater danger.

Fight alongside these three courageous forces for freedom in all-new
ion-packed novels! Travel to the gloomy depths of the cold Atlantic, the
rching sands of the Sahara, and the desolate Russian plains. You'll
l the pressure and excitement building page after page, with nonstop
on that keeps you enthralled until the explosive conclusion!

w you can have all the new Gold Eagle novels delivered right your home!

You won't want to miss a single one of these exciting new action-adventures.
d you don't have to! Just fill out and mail the card at right, and we'll enter
r name in the Gold Eagle home subscription plan. You'll then receive four
nd-new action-packed books in the Gold Eagle series every other month,
vered right to your home! You'll get two **Mack Bolan** novels, one
le Team book and one **Phoenix Force**. No need to worry about sellouts
he bookstore…you'll receive the latest books by mail as soon as they come
the presses. That's four enthralling action novels every other month, featuring
hree of the exciting series included in the Gold Eagle library. Mail the card
ay to start your adventure.

EE! Mack Bolan bumper sticker.

When we receive your card we'll send your four explosive Gold Eagle
els and, absolutely FREE, a Mack Bolan "Live Large" bumper sticker! This
e, colorful bumper sticker will look great on your car, your bulletin board, or
where else you want people to know that you like to "live large." And you are
er no obligation to buy anything—because your first four books come on a
day free trial! If you're not thrilled with these four exciting books, just return
m to us and you'll owe nothing. The bumper sticker is yours to keep, FREE!

Don't miss a single one of these thrilling novels…mail the card now, while
're thinking about it. And get the Mack Bolan bumper sticker FREE as our

BOLAN FIGHTS AGAINST ALL ODDS TO DEFEND FREEDOM

Mail this coupon today!

Gold Eagle Reader Service, a division of Worldwide Library
In U.S.A.: 2504 W. Southern Avenue, Tempe, Arizona 85282
In Canada: P.O. Box 2800, Postal Station 'A', 5170 Yonge Street, Willowd
Ont. M2N 5T5

FREE! MACK BOLAN BUMPER STICKER
when you join our home subscription plan.

YES, please send me my first four Gold Eagle novels, and include my FREE Mack Bola
bumper sticker as a gift. These first four books are mine to examine free for 10 days. I
am not entirely satisfied with these books, I will return them within 10 days and owe
nothing. If I decide to keep these novels, I will pay just $1.95 per book (total $7.80). I wi
then receive the four new Gold Eagle novels every other month as soon as they come u
the presses, and will be billed the same low price of $7.80 per shipment. I understand ti
each shipment will contain two Mack Bolan novels, one Able Team and one Phoenix
Force. There are no shipping and handling or any other hidden charges. I may cancel t
arrangement at any time and the bumper sticker is mine to keep as a FREE gift, even i
do not buy any additional books.

NAME   (PLEASE PRINT)

ADDRESS   APT. N

CITY   STATE/PROV.   ZIP/POSTAL CO

Signature   (If under 18, parent or guardian must sign.) 166-BPM-PA

This offer limited to one order per household. We reserve the right to exercise discretion in
granting membership. If price changes are necessary, you will be notified.
Offer expires October 31, 1984

MB-SUI